"Hello. I ha

Levi reached for her hand, his ... anticipation.

As if her instincts were bent on betraying her, Magnolia found herself extending her hand toward his, expecting the feel of his callused fingers as they closed around hers, reveling in the warm affection Levi so freely offered. However, a dark cloud of misgiving descended upon her soul, and Magnolia jerked her hand to her side. She balled her fist into a tight knot, firmly set her lips, and turned to the pile of soiled linens stacked in the corner. She didn't dare look at him. She didn't dare ponder the smoldering passion so blatant in his eyes. She didn't dare hope that a man like Levi would continue in his warm regard upon learning the truth of her upbringing. . . .

"Have I. . .in some way offended you, Magnolia?" he asked softly.

She bit her lip as tears of bitterness stung her eyes. *No,* she wanted to yell. *No. You have done nothing. Only Uncle Cahill, the man I thought I could trust. Now I don't know if I can trust a soul. Now I don't know if anyone will even want to associate with me.*

DEBRA WHITE SMITH lives in East Texas with her husband and two small children. She is an author and speaker who pens both books and magazine articles and has twenty-five book sales to her credit, both fiction and non-fiction. Debra holds a B.A. and M.A. in English and has hundreds of thousands of books in print. Both she and her novels have been voted favorites by **Heartsong Presents** readers. *Texas Lady* is the series book to *Texas Honor* and *Texas Rose* and will soon be followed by *Texas Angel*. A portion of her earnings from her writing goes to Christian Blind Mission, International. You may visit Debra on the world wide web at www.get-set.com/debrawhitesmith.

Books by Debra White Smith

HEARTSONG PRESENTS
HP237—The Neighbor
HP284—Texas Honor
HP343—Texas Rose

Texas Lady

Debra White Smith
with Susan K. Downs

Heartsong Presents

For my friend, Susan K. Downs.

A note from the author:

I love to hear from my readers! You may correspond with me by writing:

Debra White Smith
Author Relations
PO Box 719
Uhrichsville, OH 44683

ISBN 1-57748-700-1

TEXAS LADY

All Scripture quotations are taken from the Authorized King James Version of the Bible.

Cover illustration by Kevin McCain.

PRINTED IN THE U.S.A.

prologue

(Taken from *Texas Rose*, Heartsong Presents #343)

Kate Lowell picked her way across the street full of muddy slush and opened the door to the Dogwood general store. The smells of coffee, peppermint, and new material greeted her. Kate glanced around the store lined with horse plows, bags of cornmeal, sugar, flour, and the ever-present wall of postal boxes behind the counter. Immediately she was drawn to the material table and began examining several bolts of heavy cotton, exactly the kind of material she needed for an all-purpose work dress.

Out of the corner of her eye, Kate noticed the buxom Bess Tucker about to approach her, but she stopped to help another couple, buying supplies for their kitchen. At closer observation, Kate realized the couple was Travis Campbell and his new wife, Rachel. Never in her life had Kate wanted so desperately to disappear as at that moment. She suppressed the urge to crawl under the material table, but decided to simply keep her back to them in hopes that they wouldn't notice her. The last time she saw Travis and Rachel, she and Travis broke off their engagement and she rode away, leaving him to marry the woman of his heart, Rachel Isaacs. That was the day before Kate met Mr. Adams and Drew at the train station.

To encounter Travis and Rachel now was highly awkward and embarrassing. Kate didn't even know if they were aware she was still in Dogwood. At last, she decided to simply turn around and leave without mailing her letters. She would go to the dressmaker, who usually kept material in stock, and return to mail the letters after ordering her dress. Kate whirled around to bump squarely into Rachel.

"Oh excuse me," the young redhead said politely. "I didn't realize you. . ."

She trailed off as she recognized exactly who she had bumped into—her husband's former fiancée. "Miss Lowell!" she said with faint surprise.

"Mrs. Campbell," Kate said calmly, feeling anything but calm. She stole a glance toward Travis, tall and fair, as he neared. The last time she saw him they were on friendly, although strained, terms. Kate was very much at peace about their mutual decision to break the engagement, but she hoped Mrs. Campbell in no way thought Kate was pining for Travis.

"Hello, Kate," Travis said as he neared. "We heard you were still in town. It's a delight to see you."

"Yes. . ." Kate cleared her throat and produced a shy smile. "I suppose there isn't much that goes on in Dogwood that everyone doesn't know about."

Rachel released a spontaneous giggle, and Kate eased a bit. Perhaps the flush on Mrs. Campbell's cheeks was an indicator of her happiness and security in her marriage.

Helplessly searching for any topic of conversation, Kate opened her mouth and heard herself say, "The snow must have made you as restless as it did me. I decided that after being trapped inside yesterday, I needed to get out today."

"Actually, we—Rachel needed to see Dr. Engle," Travis said, placing an arm around his wife's waist as if she were a fragile doll.

The glowing, adoring gaze Rachel threw Travis left the rest unsaid. She was most likely expecting their first child. Kate shot a furtive glance toward Rachel's waistline only to find it unaltered. Perhaps Mrs. Campbell was very early in her pregnancy. Kate hoped there were no problems.

Rachel turned her attention back to Kate. "Travis and I were thinking of sending you an invitation to dine with us one evening if—"

"That is so thoughtful of you," Kate interrupted. "But I'm so busy with the tutoring that I—"

"We understand," Travis said. And Kate knew Travis well enough to interpret the gleam in his green eyes. Such a meeting would be as uncomfortable for him as for Kate. Surprisingly, his young wife seemed the most at ease with the whole situation.

"Well, it was extremely nice to see you again," Kate said in her most refined tone. Fully prepared to gracefully exit the store, she curtsied and began walking toward the front door. But it would appear that Kate had no room for escape this day, from any situation, for when she was no more than ten feet from the doorway, it swung open and McCall Adams walked into the store. Kate trembled in astonishment. Behind her stood the man she had once agreed to marry; and in front of her stood the man she would probably dream about the rest of her life but would never marry.

Kate would have loved to pretend she didn't see McCall,

but that proved impossible, for he looked straight at her. The purposeful gleam in his dark eyes proclaimed that he had found the person for whom he was looking. "Miss Lowell," he said with a slight smile. "The hotel owner mentioned that you might be here. May I have a minute of your time, please?"

"Yes, of course," Kate said quietly. She cringed, imagining that every eye in the store must be fixed on her as she stepped onto the boardwalk with Mr. Adams. Yet a quick glance over her shoulder proved no one watched her departure. Bess Tucker hovered near Rachel and Travis as they joyfully examined a tiny bonnet, just the size to fit a baby. The two most certainly were expectant parents.

one

Dogwood, Texas
June 1886

"Maggie!" Constable Parker shouted. "Magnolia Alexander!"

Maggie's spine tensed at the note of alarm ringing in the constable's voice. What could the constable possibly want? The bell hanging on the heavy wooden door of Dogwood's general store tinkled softly as the door closed behind her. Squinting into the sun, Maggie stepped onto the boardwalk and watched while the town's lone lawman tightened the reins of his gelding. The panting horse came to a halt amid a flurry of dust. The strong smell of leather and horse flesh swirled with the dust as Maggie waited for the constable to state his business.

"Doc Engle needs you right away," he announced. "I just brought in some fella who found himself on the wrong side of a gun during a train holdup five miles outside of town. Looks like he's been beat up pretty bad, too. I think he was throw'd from the train while it was still movin'. I've got to round up a posse to try and find—"

"I'll hurry right over," Maggie interrupted with uncustomary abruptness. Juggling the numerous packages and her worn reticule, she clutched her heavy skirt and darted down the boardwalk in an unladylike sprint.

In seconds, the young nurse stepped into the doctor's

office, heavy with the scent of kerosene and antiseptic. As warm perspiration trickled down her temples, she dropped her packages on a nearby table and untied the sash of her calico sunbonnet. With a flip of her wrist, she tossed the headpiece atop the packages. Instinctively, she grabbed that forever-defiant strand of blond hair and shoved it under the confines of her bun.

"Of all days for a good ol' Texas heat wave," Maggie complained into the stifling air. Leaning against the door, she paused to catch her breath and prepare herself for the task ahead.

As her eyes adjusted from summer sunshine to the dimness of oil lamps, she noticed Dr. Engle in the examination room. The dedicated physician, intently tending to his motionless patient, paused for a brief glance of Maggie as she stepped to his side.

"It looks like he's taken a bullet to the shoulder," the good doctor whispered. "From the looks of him, this man's gonna have a fight on his hands just to stay alive. He's already lost quite a bit of blood. Maggie, bring me some fresh water. Then gather as many clean bandages as we have around here. I'm afraid we'll need them all."

Maggie peered over the doctor's shoulder for a glimpse of the unconscious patient. Her stomach lurched as she turned away from the nauseating sight and smell of fresh blood. In exasperation, Magnolia wondered how long she would be a nurse before growing accustomed to blood. As usual, she fought off feelings of inadequacy, of doubt, of anxiety. After two years as a nurse, Maggie was losing patience with her own queasiness. Suppressing her stomach's churning, she scurried off to fulfill the doctor's orders.

She was en route to deliver a second tray of bandages when the front door burst open. An anxious Travis Campbell and his expectant wife, Rachel, stepped over the threshold.

Oh, dear Lord, Maggie pleaded silently as she took in Rachel's pale face. *Rachel's baby can't be coming now. It's much too early.* But her prayers were interrupted as Travis bolted forward.

"Constable Parker told me I should look here for my brother. Is he here? Is he hurt? How bad is it?" As the barrage of questions continued, Travis paused just long enough to politely pull the wide-brimmed hat from his head.

A sense of relief flooded Maggie. The Campbells were not here regarding Rachel or her unborn child. However, a whole new set of concerns replaced Maggie's short-lived relief. Could the unconscious man be Travis Campbell's brother? Should Magnolia be the one to report his grave condition? What if the patient were someone else? She certainly did not want to bring undue stress upon the expecting Rachel.

Attempting to display an air of composure, Maggie motioned for the distraught couple to sit on the muddled-brown horsehair sofa that filled one wall of the office. Feigning nonchalance, she walked to the examination room's open door and pulled the handle until she heard a firm click. Thankfully, the Campbells had been too preoccupied to notice the activity in the next room. Positioning a chair in front of the troubled couple, Maggie sat facing Rachel and simply raised her eyebrows questioningly. With no further prompting, Rachel launched into a detailed explanation of the day's tragic events.

"We were waitin' at the station for Travis's brother, Levi, to arrive on this morning's ten-thirty train from El Paso," Rachel began, her pale brown eyes wide with worry. "But it didn't come and it didn't come. Of course, you know the train is often delayed, so we weren't all that concerned—especially when we finally heard it coming down the tracks around noon or so."

Maggie nodded as Rachel forged ahead. "Then when the train stopped, passengers began to climb off and run to their family members. They were all visibly shaken. The women were cryin'. And we heard someone mention a holdup. We were anxious to get the news firsthand from Levi, but he never got off the train. Just as Travis was going in search of the conductor, Constable Parker approached us."

Maggie. Magnolia Alexander. The constable's intimidating shouts replayed in Maggie's mind as she thought back to their earlier encounter. She could easily imagine the Campbells' growing sense of fear at the approach of the constable's imposing figure.

She wondered if a constable ever got to deliver good news. From Maggie's perspective, every time the constable arrived, bad news usually trailed close behind. Maggie reached over and patted Rachel's hand in a heartfelt gesture of sympathy.

At last, Travis was able to add to his wife's vivid recollections with a reasonable degree of composure. "The constable said that, according to the accounts given by other passengers, a male passenger attempted to thwart a holdup. But the bandits shot him and threw him from the moving train. And, believe it or not, the robbers were apparently two women. Can you imagine that? What kind of a woman would hold up a train?"

Rachel flipped her auburn French braid over her shoulder and nervously rose to pace toward the window. Maggie, assuming the low couch was uncomfortable for a woman with child, stood to offer her straight-backed chair. Rachel merely waved her hand in protest. However, her fidgeting left Maggie all the more tense. She crossed the room and poured them each a glass of spring water from a crockery pitcher as Rachel continued.

"Some cattlemen who saw the man bein' thrown from the train went after Constable Parker. By then, the train had stopped a ways down the track. When the constable realized how bad off the man was, he prepared to rush him here. The constable told the train conductor that he'd meet up with him at the station. He asked that no passengers be allowed to leave the station platform once they arrived in town."

Maggie handed Rachel and Travis the mugs of water and waited as they gulped the liquid.

"The constable sought us out at the station as soon as he'd had a chance to go over the passenger list with the conductor," Rachel said. "Evidently, the injured man is Levi. All the other passengers have been accounted for. We rushed over as soon as we—"

"Can we see Levi?" Travis stood and gripped his hat all the tighter. "If he's here, we simply must be allowed to see him! Can you tell us his condition?" He nervously grabbed a handful of his wheat-colored hair as though attempting to extract the mental torment from his brain. "Where's Dr. Engle? Can we talk to him?"

Typical for such a hot day, Maggie's head began to throb with the beginnings of a blinding headache. The added pressure of handling this situation only added to the pounding in her temples. Part of her wanted to tell the Campbells the injured man was most likely their relative. But a professional voice, honed by Dr. Engle, cautioned her that he might very well not be the man for whom they searched. "Dr. Engle *is* with a patient right now," she replied as she backed toward the examination room. "If you will excuse me for a moment, I'll ask him when he thinks he'll be available to see you." She slipped quickly into the room and closed the door before either of the Campbells had time to respond.

Maggie turned toward the grandfatherly doctor in time to catch him smiling at her. "I overheard snatches of your conversation," he said, walking to the basin of clean water and washing his hands. "You did a superb job of maintaining a level head under pressure. Handling distraught family members can sometimes be the most difficult assignment of the medical profession."

"Thank you," Magnolia said, assuming she must have sounded much more controlled than she felt.

"As for my work in here," Dr. Engle continued, "it appears that I've done about all I can do for the patient. We'll have to leave the rest in the hands of the Great Physician. Why don't I go out and speak to the Campbells while you stand watch over our fallen hero?"

Maggie hoped her enthusiasm over relinquishing her duties with the distraught Campbells wasn't too obvious. While Dr. Engle left the room to greet Travis and Rachel, she settled herself onto a chair next to the patient.

After the upheaval of the last hour, she enjoyed the room's serenity. With a cleansing breath, Maggie rubbed her temples and prayed that the pounding would diminish as she watched the gentle rise and fall of the blankets covering the unconscious man. She reflected on the extent of his injuries and each new breath seemed to whisper the arrival of another miracle. Magnolia surveyed his bruised, swollen face, trying to imagine what he had looked like before the beating. No matter how hard she tried, she couldn't see a resemblance between Travis Campbell and this tall, thin man. Except for his weathered, bronze skin, Maggie's imagination placed her patient behind the desk of an East Coast lawyer's office rather than herding cows on the Texas range.

Travis Campbell was a big man, well suited for a rancher's life. This man's straight brown hair, matted with dried blood, looked nothing like Travis's thick shock of tawny blond. Of course, she couldn't tell if his eyes sparkled with the same emerald green flame that jumped in Travis's eyes. Were they really brothers?

Maggie chuckled softly as she recalled the time that Travis burst into the church and put a halt to Rachel's impending marriage to Samuel James. She wondered if this man had inherited his brother's tendency toward impulsiveness. That might explain his quick and gutsy reaction to the train robbery.

Dr. Engle's voice just outside the door stirred Maggie from her reverie. In lighthearted banter, the good doctor teased, "Travis, I seem to recall that my first introduction to you came in this office—and under similar circumstances."

Maggie remembered now. She had been home in bed

with a bad cold and of no use to Dr. Engle when Travis Campbell limped into town battered and bruised. Apparently, a man intent on stealing Travis's identity had beaten him up, tied him to a tree, and left him to die. Were *all* the Campbell men destined to jump, feet-first, into trouble?

"Now, I'll let you in for just a moment, Travis," Dr. Engle warned. "But remember, you are not to utter a sound. We *cannot* allow you to disturb the patient. He desperately needs his rest. Just give me a quick nod if this man is definitely your brother. Do you understand?" Dr. Engle opened the door, and Travis entered the room alighted with lanterns and sunshine.

Leaving her seat, Maggie allowed Travis to tiptoe next to the bed. He took one look at the injured man, then immediately nodded his affirmation to Dr. Engle. At this signal, Dr. Engle motioned for Maggie to meet him at the door. "I'll stay here with Travis for a minute," the physician whispered. "Why don't you go out and sit with Rachel. I think she could use your company." Maggie quietly eased out of the room.

"It is Levi, isn't it?" Rachel asked as she adjusted her summer shawl to cover her expanding figure.

"Rachel, I'm. . .I'm sure he's going to be. . .be all right," Maggie sputtered. "You couldn't ask for a better doctor to look after him than Doc Engle. And I wouldn't be surprised if the Reverend didn't already have the ladies' prayer circle on their knees."

"Levi was to be the first of Travis's relatives to visit us," Rachel said, fretting with the tangled tassels on her shawl. "I've yet to meet any of Travis's kin. And I so wanted to make a good first impression. We didn't offer him much of a welcome, did we?"

A flurry of activity out the front window caught Maggie's attention. Dust clouds rose in front of the jailhouse as a dozen or more men on stomping horses circled the constable. Maggie jerked her head toward the window. "Looks like Constable Parker has a great welcoming committee lined up for those women robbers—if they can find them."

As she spoke, Maggie scanned the faces of the gathering posse in hopes of catching a glimpse of Uncle Cahill, her only living relative. Perhaps he was out in the horse pasture and hadn't heard the news of the train holdup. One thing for sure, he would be hoppin' mad when he learned he missed a chance to hunt down and capture a couple of female outlaws.

Dr. Engle's firm footfalls distracted Maggie and Rachel from their observation of the gathering posse. "Maggie, I would appreciate it if you would stay with our patient while I walk over to Dotty's Café with the Campbells. They never had a chance to eat lunch. Regardless of the circumstances, Rachel must eat and take proper care of herself if we want this baby to be as strong and handsome as its papa."

Out of the corner of her eye, Maggie noticed Rachel's heat-flushed face turn a dark shade of crimson. *Surely Dr. Engle knows he should never refer to a woman's delicate condition in mixed company*, Maggie thought as the two men ushered Rachel out the door. *Has his wife been dead and gone so long that he has forgotten how to handle a lady's sensitive nature?*

She scurried back to the bedside of her unconscious charge and noiselessly set about the task of tidying up the mess Dr. Engle had left behind. With an armload of bloodied towels, Maggie headed for the hallway that led to the doctor's adjoining home. She needed to immediately set these things to soak in the kitchen's large washtub if there was to be any hope of removing the stains.

Just as Maggie reached the door, a low moan filtered from the bed. Dropping the towels where she stood, Maggie gingerly made her way back to the bedside. Although his eyes remained closed, his arm twitched. Well, the towels would simply have to stain. She certainly couldn't leave the room now.

Maggie positioned her chair no more than a foot from Levi's pillow so that she could observe his every move. Almost afraid to blink, she intently gazed at his face. *He certainly must be quite handsome without the swollen cuts and bruises*, she determined as she studied him. *I wonder what his eyes look like. I just hope and pray that he lives to see from them again!*

As if on cue, Levi blinked. His eyes sparkled with the same emerald green fire that danced in his brother Travis's eyes. Startled, Maggie simply held his gaze.

"Are. . .you. . .my guardian angel?" he rasped.

"Excuse me?" Maggie replied, not at all certain what she had heard.

"Are y–you my guardian angel," he whispered, this time a bit stronger.

"Why, no," Maggie stuttered, "I'm Magnolia Alexander."

"I. . .I am c–c–certain. Certain you m–m–must be an angel," Levi replied. "And I. . .I am undoubtedly in. . .in Heaven." His weak, stammering speech halted just long enough for him to draw a deep breath. "A face as beauti–

beautiful as yours doesn't be–be–belong on earth." Levi managed a weak smile, then winked at his angel of mercy as though he were a flirtatious schoolboy at a barn dance rather than a man freshly snatched from the jaws of death.

two

Maggie's face heated as she groped for a proper response. She might have slapped him if he weren't already beaten and bruised. *What gall!* Apparently Dr. Engle wasn't the only man who didn't know the proper thing to say in the presence of a lady.

"Sir," Maggie impulsively responded, "with manners like yours, it's unlikely you would find yourself on Heaven's shore. Consider yourself fortunate that you are still on this earth! I shall choose to assume that the morphine Dr. Engle administered must be wearing off and has left you a bit delirious. Surely under normal circumstances you would keep such comments to yourself!"

Despite her stern countenance and harsh words, Maggie couldn't stop the giddiness from washing over her. This brave man with his penetrating eyes thought she was beautiful! Maggie dared not look at him again for if she did, he might easily see the rush of pleasure his unexpected, flagrant flirtation had caused her as Mr. Campbell smiled drowsily. She rose and crossed the room, where she began to once again gather the soiled towels.

"Mr. Campbell, unless you have any pressing needs, I will momentarily excuse myself and put these things in the washtub." Her pale blue skirt swishing, Maggie glanced over her shoulder only to see the patient once more in the deep throes of slumber.

Upon reaching the kitchen, Maggie gave the soiled towels a cursory scrubbing with a bar of homemade lye soap, then dunked them in the washtub full of cool well water. "Mr. Campbell is sure to be hungry soon," she said to herself while she dried her hands on her starched apron. A skillet of cornbread sat on the table next to the cast-iron stove and Maggie cut a generous butter-smeared triangle.

The sound of rattled snoring greeted Maggie as she neared Levi's bedside. Frankly, she was glad that she didn't have to look Levi in the eyes again. Although her head's pounding had indeed subsided, she relished the chance to relax and think through the day's events. Easing herself into the bedside chair, she gently smoothed her patient's covers.

Allowing the room's peaceful ambience to embrace her, Maggie once more puzzled over not seeing Uncle Cahill among the posse. She resolved to soon travel out to the farm and check on him. Missing out on a posse wasn't like him. She really hoped he wasn't ill.

Before Maggie had a chance to further worry, Dr. Engle and the Campbells rattled at the door as they returned from their meal. The moment Maggie stepped into the outer office to greet them, the wafting aroma of Dotty's corned beef and cabbage assailed her senses. Maggie detested cabbage and the offensive smell left her stomach in knots. Excitedly, she whispered the news of Levi's waking, leaving out the details of their embarrassing conversation. "He seems to be resting as comfortably as can be expected now," she concluded.

Dr. Engle patted Maggie on the shoulder sympathetically. "You've had a busy day. I'll stand watch over our patient. You head on home and get some rest. You can relieve me in the morning."

"Well," Maggie replied, "I *was* thinking that I should look in on Uncle Cahill. Mr. Campbell, would it be too much of an imposition for you and Rachel to carry me as far as his farm? That is. . . ," she glanced from the Campbells to Dr. Engle, ". . .if you're goin' home now."

"Yes," Dr. Engle said, checking the brass watch tucked in the pocket of his ebony vest. "I insist they go home. The afternoon is waning, and Rachel *must* maintain her rest."

"But Levi—" Travis said.

"Will be fine." Dr. Engle laid a calming hand on Travis's arm.

Rachel, her face less agitated than when she left for Dotty's, nodded her agreement. "If you really think so, Doctor. I believe I am in need of some rest." Wearily, she shoved her braid over her shoulder.

"Of course. Of course," Travis said like a doting knight. His somewhat relaxed countenance attested to Dr. Engle's gift for soothing the relatives of his injured patients. "We pass right by your uncle's farm, Miss Alexander. Gather your things while I take one more look at Levi. I'll meet you and Rachel at the buggy."

After scooping up her belongings from the table, Maggie held the door for Rachel and they stepped into the steaming afternoon heat.

As Maggie assisted Rachel into the black runabout, she caught sight of the stately Sarah Baker, the boardinghouse mistress who owned the home where Maggie resided. "Oh, Mrs. Baker," Maggie called toward the boardwalk, "I'm glad you happened by. I won't be joining you for supper tonight. The Campbells have graciously agreed to drive me out to visit Uncle Cahill on the farm. I should be home before dark, though."

"That will be just fine, Maggie," Mrs. Baker replied, her refined voice barely reaching louder than a whisper. "Our gentlemen boarders are all out with the posse in search of the train bandits. I had planned to just dish up a bowl of bean soup with johnnycake anyway. It will keep another day. Besides, I need to pay a call on an acquaintance this evening." The cultured Mrs. Baker, dressed in a tailored, navy blue suit, hurried past the doctor's office in the direction of the Dogwood saloon.

Rachel leaned toward Maggie, her expression full of questions. "Maggie, you are close to both Doc Engle and the Widow Baker. Surely you have some idea why they haven't spoken to each other in over three years!"

"I wish I *did* know. But neither of them will discuss the matter. It's a cryin' shame that those two can't settle their differences and get together. Miz Baker is much too young to be alone for her remaining years. And when Dr. Engle's wife passed away, I think we all agreed that he and Miz Baker would make a perfect couple."

Travis joined the women in the buggy and stepped into the conversation. "I'm just a newcomer to Dogwood, but a man would have to be blind not to notice the sparks that fly between those two," he said in his well-bred voice. "I guess you are in quite a predicament, Miss Alexander, working for one and living with the other."

Maggie shrugged. "I've just learned which subjects to avoid." She smiled. "Mainly romance."

As the bay mare pulled the buggy past Main Street's last

frame house and onto the tree-lined lane that led to the Alexander and Campbell farms, Travis and Rachel once more discussed the train robbery. However, Magnolia's mind rested less on the subject of the robbery and more on the victim, Levi Campbell, with his sparkling emerald eyes and flirtatious tongue. She forced her lips not to turn up at the improper delight his outlandish words stirred within her. In the morning, Dr. Engle fully expected her to sit with the patient. Perhaps Maggie would pay a "casual" visit to the office tonight "just to see if she could be of use."

At last, Travis pulled onto the earth-packed circle drive leading to the farmhouse. The fragrant pines filling the yard obscured the view of the white frame homestead until the buggy pulled around to the porch. A sense of nostalgia and anticipation swept over Maggie at the sight of her one-story childhood home. At the porch's east end, the green swing creaked gently on its chains as a soft breeze suggested the coming of evening. Magnolia knew without looking that notches in the doorpost charted her childhood growth.

"I do appreciate the lift, Mr. Campbell. There's no need for you to escort me in. Just drop me off right here at the door." Greeted by the deep bark of Uncle Cahill's coon-hound, Ruff, Maggie climbed out of the buggy.

But as she ascended the two steps onto the covered porch, she noticed the front door standing wide open. At once, Magnolia revisited her earlier nagging worries, worries that her beloved uncle might be ill. Could those worries have been more than unfounded apprehension? A pall of precognition seemed to drape itself around her shoulders as she stepped through the open door. "Uncle

Cahill, are you home?" she called in a trembling voice.

❧

Somewhere in the distance, a woman urged, "Wake up, Maggie! Maggie, you must wake up." The cool cloth on her forehead broke through her stupor, but her eyes refused to open. "Oh, Travis," the woman's voice came through again, "what are we goin' to do? The constable is out with the posse and Dr. Engle has his hands full with Levi."

"Unfortunately, Dr. Engle's skills aren't needed here. Cahill Alexander is dead. We might as well head back to town and bring the undertaker. But we can't leave Maggie. We'll have to get her up and take her with us. It appears that whoever killed her uncle is long gone. Still, we can't be sure—and I can't take the risk of leaving either of you behind."

"Now, get up from the floor, Rachel. I worry about you. You're in no condition to be down there. Given time, Maggie will wake up on her own. She's received a terrible shock, but she'll be all right."

The words filtering into Maggie's consciousness brought a renewed sense of terror as she remembered the moments just prior to her fainting. *Murdered. Uncle Cahill has been murdered.* Maggie blinked and looked past the vigilant Rachel to see Travis in her uncle's bedroom, gingerly placing Cahill Alexander's body on his bed. Without warning, waves of nausea crashed over Maggie. Her stomach could no longer contain its contents. She turned her head away from Rachel just in time.

When her heaving stopped, an extended groan of pure agony escaped from the depths of Maggie's soul. Grief overwhelming her, she began to sob. Her uncle Cahill was the only family she had in this world. What was she going to do? How could she go on living? Why would anyone want to kill this kind, gentle man? At this moment, Maggie wished she could die, too. *Dear God, Why? Why? Why?*

Maggie lay on the floor and sobbed until her head began to pound anew, until her throat ached, until her heart felt as if it had been twisted in two. When her initial mourning began to fade, the sniffling Rachel gently dabbed her mouth with the cool washcloth. "Oh, you poor, poor dear. You poor, poor dear."

❧

Over the next several days, word spread throughout the county of Cahill Alexander's murder. As Maggie tended to the myriad of details and decisions that accompany any death, she must have heard Rachel's words repeated at least a thousand times. "You poor dear. . .you poor, poor dear." Maggie was surrounded, day and night, by well-meaning, sympathetic townsfolk, each one expressing their own variation of the same theme, "You poor, poor dear."

After a week of listening to the entire town's commiseration, Magnolia had a compelling urge to scream—not out of anguish and grief, but from a sense of being smothered. She was thoroughly tired of being pitied. She had been condolenced to death.

Three days after her uncle's funeral, Maggie decided her status of mourning must be altered. Before climbing out of bed, she had planned her entire day. In the afternoon, she would slip out to Uncle Cahill's farm alone and sort through his things. But first, she desperately needed a diversion from these prevailing thoughts of death and sorrow, and Maggie knew just where to go to soothe her frazzled nerves. She would head over to Doc Engle's and tend to Levi Campbell. There she could avoid this oppressive sympathy and focus her attentions on someone other than herself. A shiver of excitement raced through her thoughts as she considered seeing the convalescing Mr. Campbell again. But Maggie quickly squelched her improper contemplation with a forceful reminder: *You are supposed to be in mourning. . .and you are very vulnerable right now. Guard your heart!*

Afraid of disturbing the sleeping boarders, Maggie slipped into her black mourning clothes as quietly as possible and tiptoed from the boardinghouse onto the rain-soaked boardwalk. The gray weather matched Maggie's mood. Her violent inner storms of grief had subsided, leaving her spirits surrounded by a heavy haze.

Am I doing the right thing by coming here this morning? Maggie questioned as she paused outside Dr. Engle's office. But the prospect of seeing Levi Campbell again compelled her inside.

Dr. Engle, his shoulders drooping with exhaustion, appeared genuinely startled at the sight of Maggie as she shook the rain from her umbrella and hung her reticule on the peg beside the front door. "Maggie, my dear. Why are you here?" He stroked his white mustache and pushed the spectacles up his nose, closer to his bloodshot eyes. "I can handle the responsibilities. Really, I can manage just fine for at least another day or two," he insisted. "You must take as much time as you need to recover from your recent tragedy."

"Now, let's be reasonable, Dr. Engle," Maggie asserted,

trying her dead-level best to resist the urge to cry in the face of the doctor's kind demeanor. "I can certainly help out for an hour or two. I know without asking that you at least need to make a house call out at the Williamses' farm. I insist that you run along and let me care for things around here. Might not hurt for you to lie down when you get back as well. You look like you need the rest. Besides. . . ," she clutched the book she had brought for Levi's enjoyment, "I think it will. . .will do me. . .do me good to focus on something else for. . .for a while." Magnolia blinked against her stinging eyes.

"Of course, dear," the kind doctor said, his voice oozing with fatherly understanding. In respectful silence, he began preparing his black bag.

Maggie approached Levi's door, her palms moist as she touched the cool brass knob. Only days ago, she had said her final good-byes to Uncle Cahill, the man of her past. Could Levi Campbell be the man of her future? The thought sent a tremor along her spine. In her state of mourning, Magnolia should not be experiencing such improper emotions. But even *if* Uncle Cahill had not been murdered, Levi Campbell's blatantly flirtatious references to Maggie as his angel of mercy should be enough to curtail a proper lady's interest. Nonetheless, her heart gently pounded in anticipation of seeing him again. Immediately, another thought struck her. Would Mr. Campbell even remember her? Perhaps the effects of morphine had produced his disgraceful words and Magnolia would be a stranger to him.

With a faint click, she opened the door, fully expecting to see Levi in the arms of sleep. Instead, she encountered those sparkling green eyes, a gaze of admiration, and a welcoming smile. "Well, if it isn't my angel of mercy, come to comfort me in my hour of need!"

Her face warming, Magnolia's question of whether or not he would recognize her fled through the window, opened for the morning's cool breeze. That same sparkle of mischief still stirred in his eyes and Maggie sternly inserted her bottom lip between her teeth to stop the inappropriate smile now pushing against the corners of her mouth.

At last, she mustered an offended scowl. "Mr. Campbell, I've simply come to relieve Dr. Engle so that he can make some house calls," she said primly. But deep inside, Magnolia shamelessly reveled in the attention. What would Mrs. Baker think of her? Yet despite the landlady's disapproval, Mr. Campbell certainly offered Maggie a needed respite from her real-life nightmares.

As she smoothed the covers around her patient's shoulders, Levi nodded his head in acknowledgment of her curt rebuff. "Please forgive my insensitivity, Miss Alexander." Maggie gazed into his suddenly solemn eyes and, without warning, a warm rush of affection flooded over her. Could the man behind the mischievous eyes and flirtatious tongue also possess a tender heart?

"I don't know what came over me," Levi continued with a tone of sincerity that could not possibly be feigned. "Dr. Engle shared the circumstances of the terrible tragedy you have suffered. May I offer you my most heartfelt sympathies? I'm afraid I am not too skilled in the art of conversing with a lady. You see, while my brother chose to attend college in Boston, I decided to stay on the ranch. I spend most of my days talking to the cows on my father's spread in El Paso. In all honesty, I owe you a great debt for your good care, Miss Alexander, and I shall try to behave myself from now on."

"Apology accepted, Mr. Campbell." The surge of affection increased in potency to firmly wrap Maggie in its inviting embrace. "And there is really no need to thank me. I'm just doing my job." She should not—*should not* be experiencing such emotions about a man so recently in her acquaintance. Nevertheless, the emotions continued to flow, and her knees increased their traitorous trembling with his every word.

"I'd be much obliged if you'd just call me Levi," he said, his brows arched hopefully.

Magnolia swallowed hard and made a monumental job of walking across the room toward the simple table to fill his cup from the crockery pitcher. Astounded at her ability to maintain outward composure when, inwardly, she reeled with unexpected reactions, Maggie hesitated over his request. His asking for such a familiarity so early in their acquaintance bordered on improper. However, try as she might, she couldn't keep her lips from curving upward into the faintest of smiles as she placed the thick mug in his good hand.

"I know we only just met," he said with a measure of soft triumph. "But. . ."

The bruises and scrapes still marred his face, but his freshly washed brown hair now shimmered with sun-streaked highlights. And his chiseled features suggested a lineage of nobility. He was more than your run-of-the-mill Texas cowpoke. Despite his claims of not going to college in the East, the cadence of his words suggested a man well read.

"Everyone calls me Maggie," she said, amazed that she fell into his plan so readily. But nothing in her life the last few days was "as it should be." Why should her acquaintance with Levi be any different?

"Yes. . .Maggie. I've heard the doctor refer to you by that name. Is it by chance short for. . ." He winced with pain as he tried to scoot up in the bed.

"Magnolia. It's short for Magnolia." Instantly, she added an extra pillow behind Levi's head, and he relaxed against it to slowly raise the mug to his lips.

"Magnolia is such a beautiful name, it would be a shame to shorten it," he said, eyeing her over the rim of the stoneware mug.

Her heart now palpitating wildly, Maggie stood speechless, not really knowing the appropriate way to react. Levi's unexpected tenderness caught her completely off guard. *Is God sending Levi into my life at a time when I need someone the most?* Maggie transformed this fleeting thought into a silent prayer. *Oh, Lord, could it be?*

Although more than one suitor had strongly pursued Maggie's hand in marriage, she had never been in a hurry to find a husband. She enjoyed her work too much to trade it for life as a wife just yet. Besides, not a single one of her previous beaus had created the inner turmoil now overwhelming her.

This is ridiculous, Maggie scolded herself. *Absurd. I've only seen this man twice, and here I am practically tying the knot.* By force of habit, she pushed at the wayward lock of hair that constantly aggravated her.

"Have they caught the villain who committed this heinous act, Magnolia?" Never breaking eye contact, he extended the mug to her.

Maggie slowly shook her head. "I'm afraid not. Constable Parker suspects that the same women bandits who shot you might well have been responsible for my uncle's murder. The fact that they are still on the loose makes us all mighty uneasy in these parts. But I guess I needn't tell you. I imagine you won't really rest well at night until they are safely behind bars."

"Humph." Levi grimaced in agreement. "I suppose you're right about that. I am curious to know just what would make any woman turn to such a violent life of crime. Those two scoundrels just prove once again—women will always be a mystery to me!" The fiery sparkle of impishness returned to Levi's eyes. "One thing's for sure, they may be women, but they are certainly no ladies. They don't deserve the same respect afforded one as genteel as you."

Maggie's face heated at his blatant flattery, but she didn't feel compelled to make him stop. In fact, she swallowed a rising giggle and secretly wished he would continue. Levi was only too happy to oblige her unspoken desire.

"Magnolia, judging from my first impressions, your uncle must have been a very special man to have reared a lovely lady such as yourself. If you feel up to the task, I'd be honored if you'd tell me about him."

These words were the only prompting Maggie needed to launch her into a lengthy litany of her uncle's attributes.

❧

Captivated, Levi simply nodded his encouragement for Maggie to continue. *I wonder what it would be like to have someone as beautiful as Magnolia Alexander so deeply devoted to you?* If Levi had stopped to analyze his feelings, he would have recognized a slight twinge of jealousy over the fierce loyalty Magnolia held for her deceased uncle Cahill. *What would it take for her to transfer such devotion to me?*

Every minute that ticked off the mantel clock wrapped him deeper in enthrallment over the beauty before him. Her peach-colored lips. Her expressive blue eyes. Her ladylike manners. Undoubtedly, Magnolia Alexander was a woman of integrity. An overwhelming urge to gently brush a strand of blond hair out of Magnolia's eyes was squelched only by his injuries and his earlier promise of propriety.

Never had Levi so blatantly flirted with a lady, but something about Miss Magnolia Alexander unleashed his tongue and filled the air with the sweet, poetic words he had often written or read but had never voiced. No one except his parents knew he read poetry while on the cattle trail. But at last, all those lines of iambic pentameter, long locked into his heart, seemed to be finding expression with this angelic creature before him.

An hour later, Dr. Engle's return ended Magnolia's sweet reminisces. And Levi fought to mask his disappointment. In those sixty short minutes, Levi had received a succinct summary of Maggie's life history and a clear understanding of the important part her dearly beloved uncle Cahill had played in her upbringing. With Dr. Engle attending Levi's wound, a startling supposition consumed his thoughts. *Just suppose. Could it be? Dear God, is Magnolia Alexander the answer to the countless prayers I've prayed under the prairie stars?*

"I know it's a lot to ask of you at this sad time, Magnolia," Levi blurted as Maggie prepared to leave. "But, would you mind coming back for a bit tomorrow? I truly enjoy your company. This visit has done me more good than any of Doc Engle's medicines."

Dr. Engle gently applied a clean bandage and produced a halfhearted grumble as his bloodshot eyes widened in speculation.

"No disrespect intended, Doc, but. . ." Levi eyed the flushing Maggie and didn't attempt to hide one ounce of the admiration flowing from his soul.

Maggie, smiling in pleasured reserve, nodded her agreement.

three

Even as Maggie agreed to Levi's request, she scolded herself for her brazen openness with this virtual stranger. She had never revealed so much about herself to such a recent acquaintance. What had gotten into her? Surely it was her grief, expressing itself in this unexpected way. Still, she couldn't help but look forward to another opportunity to sit with the convalescing "fallen hero," as Dr. Engle had dubbed him. With a gentle sweeping motion, Maggie smoothed his sheets one last time and gave Levi's pillow a little pat as she turned and walked toward the door.

"Our patient appears much improved," Dr. Engle commented as he escorted Maggie to the outer office and she gathered her things. His teasing tone suggested that the doctor was baiting her to disclose her private thoughts. Had her attraction to the patient been as obvious as Levi's admiration for her?

Maggie refused to take the bait. "Why, yes, Dr. Engle," she said practically. "How could Mr. Campbell help but improve under your good care? Now, if you don't mind, I really must excuse myself until tomorrow. I have an important errand to run."

"You know, Maggie," Dr. Engle chuckled as she stepped out the door, opening her umbrella against the drizzling rain, "laughter and love are the best medicines for any injury, whether of the body *or* soul."

Averting her gaze, Maggie feigned a deaf ear to his sage advice. But inside, her broken heart, still palpitating with pain from the loss of her uncle, hungered for more of Levi's laughter, and perhaps. . .his love.

❧

A gentle shower continued to fall as Maggie hitched her wagon to the front porch where she had spent many long hours sipping lemonade. The old homestead seemed to open its arms to her as it had in years gone by. She had informed no one of the nature or destination of her errand. Had anyone known, they would have surely stopped her or insisted on coming along. But this was a job that Maggie simply must do alone.

Uncle Cahill's farm would be sold. Jed Sweeney, who owned the Dogwood saloon, as well as a string of saloons throughout the frontier, had been passing through town in order to check on his business. He approached Maggie about possibly buying the farm, making a solid offer. Respectfully offering his condolences, the saloon owner asked if he might return in another week or two to inquire of her decision.

The vices promoted through Sweeney's saloons repulsed Maggie, and she didn't relish the idea of someone like him taking over the place. But Maggie possessed neither the skills nor the desire required to run the farm. Unlike Rachel Campbell, who ran her father's ranch after his death, Magnolia simply lacked the spunk to undertake such an endeavor. Her strengths lay in comforting the sick, not managing an estate. Therefore, if no other buyers appeared, she would consider Mr. Sweeney's offer. Fortunately, God had granted them a wet summer so far, so Magnolia had turned all the livestock out to pasture, where they would find plenty to eat and drink from the fertile countryside and the farm pond. For now, they would survive. Besides, Uncle Cahill's hired hands had agreed to continue their usual chores and Travis Campbell graciously offered to keep an eye on the neighboring Alexander farm. But soon, the property and livestock would need the care someone like Jed Sweeney could provide.

In order to get the house ready for sale, she needed to clear out all of Uncle Cahill's personal possessions and those few items of her own that remained in her childhood home. Her uncle had been a man of little material wealth, so the task wouldn't take long.

Maggie was eager to finish this unwelcome chore and put her life back in order. Still, her emotions boiled to the surface as she walked through the door into the front room. Blood stubbornly stained the wood floors where Uncle Cahill had lain. Magnolia skittered as quickly as she could across the room and into her uncle's bedroom. She preferred to save the front room cleaning for last. Perhaps by then she could handle the ominous task.

Surely, she had made more decisions in the past three days than in all her previous twenty-three years. At every turn, well-meaning friends surrounded her, giving her advice and counsel, whether she had asked for it or not. Today, despite the heart-wrenching pain of the task, Maggie desired solitude.

The stiff skirts of Maggie's borrowed black moiré dress rustled around her as she knelt and opened the lid to the chest at the end of the pine bed. Maggie inhaled deeply, drawing in the pungent aroma of cedar from the open chest. Sighing, she lifted out the first item. Maggie knew before looking what the satin-wrapped package contained. The Alexander family Bible. Her mother, using meticulous penmanship, had recorded their brief family history in its front pages prior to her death. The first page recorded the marriage details of Maggie's parents, Jeremiah Taylor Alexander and Rose Marie Simpson Alexander on January 29, 1860, in Canal Town, Ohio.

Under the heading "Births," three entries were inscribed: *Twin sons, Curtis Jeremiah Alexander and Taylor Cahill Alexander, born November 10, 1861.* And *Magnolia Marie Alexander, born May 1, 1863.*

On the tear-stained page entitled "Deaths," Maggie's finger instinctively traced over the names written in her mother's delicate hand: *Curtis Jeremiah Alexander, died November 11, 1861. May his sweet, innocent soul rest secure in Jesus' arms. Taylor Cahill Alexander, died November 19, 1861. We shall understand it better by and by.*

The words were few, but even twenty-five years later, her mother's grief seemed to seep from the page. Surely Maggie's mother had loved her with the same fierce devotion she had heaped upon her firstborn twins. Maggie couldn't really remember her mother's love, yet her heart ached at the loss of the relationship she never experienced. All Maggie's knowledge of her mother sprang from this chest of mementos: the Bible, a diary, two photographs, and a threadbare, china-faced doll. Rose Alexander's journal chronicled their short-lived journey as settlers headed for the western frontier. The two faded photographs hinted at the strong resemblance Maggie now shared with her mother: one of Jeremiah and Rose Alexander on their wedding day; the other of a two-year-old Maggie and her mother. The same light hair. The same fine-boned features. The same petite frame.

Magnolia pulled her mother's suede-bound journal out of its hallowed space in the chest. As a teenager, she had practically memorized the crinkled pages. From the reading and rereading of its now-familiar scrawl, Maggie had fallen in love with these people whom history recorded as her parents. The words written there were not profound or particularly insightful. Her mother had written mostly of the challenges and hardships of their frontier travels. Yet her words provided Maggie with a sense of connection to her heritage. The handwritten accounts gave life and breath, flesh and blood to the mother and father who died before Maggie's memories began.

Maggie flipped to the last entry, dated May 1, 1866.

Our precious Magnolia now sleeps in the wagon with the new doll we presented her in celebration of her third birthday. At such a tender age, she is only beginning to understand just what a "birthday" is. But she clapped her hands and squealed with delight when her papa brought out the package containing her gift. We had kept the precious birthday surprise carefully hidden since purchasing the doll on the day of our departure from Westport.

I do regret that neither my own parents nor Jeremiah's lived long enough to know our little angel. Maggie possesses such a gentle disposition. She brings joy to our difficult journey. I often think back to the time when we lost the twins and how I begged God to give us more children. Now, like Samuel's mother, Hannah, I can say, "For this child I prayed; and the Lord hath given me my petition which I asked of him."

I must close and get some rest, for we must start out early tomorrow morning. Sometime during the night, Gertrude, our milk cow, wandered off. We had to remain behind and search for her when the rest of the wagon train broke camp. Cahill and Jeremiah found the wayward animal within a few hours, but we need to travel a good many miles tomorrow if we hope to catch up with the others again before they leave Fort Dodge, as is our plan.

Despite our hardships, when I consider my good husband, his kind brother, Cahill, and our little Magnolia, I give thanks to the Lord for His many gifts to me. My heart echoes the verse I read today in the Psalms, which says, "The lines are fallen unto me in pleasant places; yea, I have a goodly heritage."

"Yea, I have a goodly heritage," Maggie said out loud. Long ago she had claimed this verse of scripture, Psalm 16:6, as her life's motto. The claim had proven true. For, despite the fact that her parents were killed in a calamitous accident the day after her mother wrote of this psalm, her uncle Cahill had provided a strong Christian example and stable home. Though he, too, was now gone, he had left her with a rich heritage of faith.

"Oh, Lord, may I do nothing to disgrace my family's name," Magnolia prayed as she gently sorted through the chest's remaining clothing that had once belonged to her parents.

By the time she finished going through her parents' things, dust-laden spears of sunlight shot through the bedroom window, dispelling any vestiges of the day's rain. *I must work faster if I hope to finish this job today,* Maggie thought, ignoring the hunger pangs assailing her. She hadn't culled a single item from the contents of the chest. Somehow she would find a place in her room at Mrs. Baker's for the cedar box and all its treasures.

Maggie turned her attentions to the desk adjacent to her uncle's bed. The rolltop compartments held a hodgepodge of papers: livestock bills of sale, receipts for farm supplies, and letters, all yellowed with age. Expecting to find more of the same in the forever stubborn desk drawer, she gave it the usual yank required to ensure its opening.

Instead of aging receipts and letters, she found a wax-sealed parchment package tied in blue ribbon with "Magnolia Alexander" emblazoned on the front. Maggie lifted the package from the drawer and held it to her nose. The paper still held the scent of her uncle's work gloves, and her eyes stung with the memory.

Suppressing the urge to cry, Maggie untied the ribbon then broke the wax seal. The stiff parchment fell open to reveal a tattered "Wanted" poster and a thick letter, written in her uncle's unmistakable staccato script. "My Dearest Magnolia," the letter began.

Puzzled, Maggie turned her attentions first to the poster. The sketch of the wanted man bore a striking resemblance to a younger Uncle Cahill. But the poster announced a one-thousand-dollar reward for the dead-or-alive return of a stagecoach bandit by the name of James Calloway. As Maggie studied the poster's fine print, her heart began to pound wildly.

Wanted:
Dead or Alive.
James Calloway, stagecoach bandit,
wanted for the armed robbery of a stagecoach in
Ford County, Kansas, on May 2, 1866.
If you have information that might assist in the arrest
of this armed and dangerous criminal,
contact the nearest U.S. Marshall.

May 2, 1866. The day her parents' Conestoga wagon overturned on the steep bank of the Arkansas River, killing them both instantly. Her uncle Cahill had retold the events of that fatal day to Maggie on countless occasions, yet not once had he mentioned anything about a stagecoach holdup. May 2, 1866. Was it just a curious parallel that the date of the holdup was the date of her parents' death—and in the same Kansas county? Could the familiar face on this wanted poster have had anything to do with the tragic events of that day? Surely it was all just a strange coincidence that the featured criminal resembled the man who had raised her. To her knowledge, Uncle Cahill had never been one to keep secrets. Even so, a sense of foreboding blanketed Maggie like a stifling cloud, bent on snuffing out her very breath.

Visions of the careening Conestoga wagon played in Magnolia's mind. She still bore a slight scar above her right eye to prove that she had been there. Yet as graphic as her mental images, Maggie realized that her memories of the fateful accident did not all come from first-person recollections. At age three, Maggie had been too young to truly remember the tragedy. But at Maggie's insistence, Uncle Cahill had recounted the story so many times that his memories eventually became her own.

The beloved uncle's oft-repeated accounts corroborated with Maggie's mother's journal. Jeremiah and Rose Alexander had decided to pick up their Ohio roots and head for the western frontier. When Jeremiah invited his younger brother, Cahill, to accompany them, he jumped at the chance. He was always on the lookout for a new adventure. The Alexander boys used every cent of their inheritance from their parents' estate to prepare what they needed for the journey and a new life out west. They had a sturdy wagon built especially for rugged travel. Together, they planned to homestead a piece of the untamed West. They would simply set out on the Santa Fe Trail until they came to a place that felt like "home." Kansas. Colorado. New Mexico. Or points beyond.

When they reached Westport, Missouri, the Alexanders joined up with a wagon train in hopes of minimizing the dangers they would meet along the way. But one night on the Kansas plains, their milk cow, Gertie, wandered off. The Alexander family had to pull their wagon out of the train in order to search for the wayward bovine.

"Your mama insisted on our searching for that confounded cow!" Maggie could hear her uncle's booming voice echoing through her mind. "Your mama, she'd say, 'my little Magnolia needs her milk and I won't go another mile without ol' Gertie.' " Uncle Cahill's voice would always soften about then and he'd say, "But Maggie, you needed a mother a heap more than you needed milk. I wish we'd ajust kept on agoin' that day."

According to Uncle Cahill, the accident occurred just after they'd broken camp and were setting out onto the trail, skirting a deep embankment on the river. Rose sat beside Jeremiah on the buckboard as he drove the mule team; three-year-old Maggie still slept in the canvas-covered wagon behind them. Uncle Cahill said he had been riding his horse alongside the wagon when he saw a water moccasin fall from a willow tree. The poisonous snake landed on the back of the wagon's lead mule, instantly sinking its fangs into the mule's tender neck muscles. The startled mule bolted, and the entire mule team took off down the trail in a dead run, the wagon bouncing wildly in their wake. Uncle Cahill had been powerless to stop the panicked mules before the wagon hit a rut and toppled over the edge of the embankment.

The wagon flipped over and over before coming to rest in the shallow waters of the Arkansas, pinning Rose and Jeremiah under its weight. Maggie had been thrown clear of the tumbling Conestoga near the top of the embankment, suffering only minor cuts and scrapes. But her parents were dead, gone before Uncle Cahill could descend the slope and come to their aid.

I am an orphan now. The thought left Maggie with an overwhelming sense of loneliness. Even though she had been orphaned at age three, this reality had never settled into her soul for Uncle Cahill had filled the gaps. But now, without Uncle Cahill, she felt truly alone in this world, an orphan in every sense of the word.

Tears sprang afresh in Maggie's eyes, yet she once more refused to vent her grief. Once the sobs started, they often lasted hours. She would survive this somehow, by the grace of God. What was the psalm that Reverend Eakin had quoted her yesterday? Something along the lines of, "A father of the fatherless, and a judge of the widows, is God in his holy habitation."

Well, Lord, this fatherless child needs You desperately now. One lone tear slid down Maggie's cheek and spattered onto Uncle Cahill's unread letter. Carefully, she blotted the tears that smeared the ink in their miniature puddles.

"*My dearest Magnolia,*" Maggie read, through blurry eyes. She tenderly clutched the letter and eased herself into a straight-backed chair.

In all likelihood, if you are reading this letter, I am either behind bars or have gone on to meet my Maker. Precious Maggie, let me begin by saying that no parent could love a child any more than I love you. You brought only joy and happiness into my life. There was never a moment when I was not proud of you. Your mama and papa would have been proud, too, to see the beautiful young lady you have become. I have done my dead-level best to bring you up like they would have wanted. If you don't mind me sayin so myself, I think I done a pretty good job of it, seeing how you have turned out and all. But, I figure you already know how I feel bout you. I've got another reason for writing this letter. You see, dear child, I have a confession to make. Many times over the years, I tried to come clean with you, but I would always chicken. I just could not face hurting you or disappointing you in any way. Even now, as I write, I am beggin God to help you understand.

My precious Maggie, it is with a heavy heart that I must tell you that I am not your real uncle. The dark secret I have carried with me these many years must now come to light. I pray that you will forgive me for not confessin sooner.

Your real uncle, Cahill Alexander, died alongside your parents on that fateful day in May. As you have probably already guessed from the enclosed poster, I was nothing more than a scoundrel and a thief in those days. My real name is James Calloway.

Now, before you get the wrong idea, let me hurry and say that I did not mean to harm or kill your family that day. They truly did die when their wagon rolled down an embankment into the Arkansas River. But it weren't no snake that frightened the mules that day. It was me—making my getaway after holding up that stage.

four

"Maggie! Magnolia Alexander!" Maggie jumped in surprise as Constable Parker's familiar voice broke through her reading. She stood horrified as she stared at the remaining pages of Uncle Cahill's letter and the incriminating wanted poster.

She could not let Constable Parker see this now. Not until she had a chance to sort it all out herself. She simply was not prepared to answer any questions. Maggie sprang into action. Rolling the documents into a scroll, she shoved them to the bottom of the open cedar chest and slammed the lid shut just as the constable's shadow darkened the bedroom door.

"My dear Miss Alexander," the constable said as he removed his straw hat. "May I ask just what on earth are you doin' out here all alone? The Widow Baker is nearly beside herself with worry. Why, she was so concerned, she even went ahuntin' you at Doc Engle's, and you know how those two avoid each other like the plague." His weathered face shone with compassion as he stroked his dundreary whiskers. "Your uncle's killers are still on the loose, remember. You can't go traipsin' around the countryside by yourself. You're just askin' for more trouble."

"Constable Parker, I assure you, sir, it was never my intent to alarm or worry anyone. Please forgive me for causing you to come all this way. Actually, I didn't expect to be here this long. I lost all track of time."

"Now, Miss Alexander." The constable's leathery countenance softened all the more as Maggie's eyes burned with unshed tears. "I'm not aimin' to be unkind. I know you've suffered more in these past few days than a soul ought to suffer in a lifetime. It's just that I'd feel so awful if somethin' were to happen to you. I understand your need to be alone. But you'd best be waitin' until I have my hands on those no-goods who killed your uncle and left that Campbell fella for dead before you venture out here by yourself again. Remember, there are criminals runnin' around these parts."

He's worried about protecting me from criminals around these parts? Maggie thought as the lawman finished his gentle scolding. *Constable Parker doesn't know I've spent most of my life under the same roof with one!* She masked her disillusioned thoughts behind a sad smile. Despite her attempts to lighten her countenance, she couldn't achieve more than the melancholic grin. "I suppose you are right, as always, Constable. I promise you—I won't venture out of town alone again until the murderers are in your custody."

"Well, all right, then. Is there somethin' I can help you do since I'm here?"

Maggie enlisted the constable's help in dragging the cedar chest from the bedroom and, with a good deal of effort, they managed to lift it onto the wagon's flatbed.

"My goodness, girl," Constable Parker exclaimed as he wiped the sweat from his brow with a soiled bandanna. "What are you totin' in here? Gold bars?"

"Just a box of memories, Constable," Maggie replied listlessly as she contemplated Uncle Cahill's revealing letter beneath the layers of her parents' treasures. The cedar box held memories, all right. Memories of love. . .memories of respect. . .memories of deceit. The beginnings of slow-burning anger ignited within Magnolia. Anger and frustration. Bitterness and shame.

Preoccupied, the constable didn't even acknowledge Maggie's disturbed demeanor. Instead, he pointed to the coonhound, Ruff, who lay dreaming under one of the yard's pine trees. "Say, Magnolia. What plans do you have for that there huntin' dog? I could use a good sniffer like him."

"Consider him yours, Constable, as payment for your kind assistance to me today. Perhaps ol' Ruff can help you find those felons before they do any more harm."

Stepping back inside the house, Maggie rushed from room to room, filling a crate with the remaining items she felt were important to keep. Still stinging from the disturbing revelations of her uncle's letter, she forced herself to pack the framed photograph of the two of them at Maggie's eighth-grade graduation. *He's not my uncle, this impostor named Calloway. He's no kin to me at all!* Nonetheless, her traitorous heart cried out for the man who had showered her with love and spoiled her as if he were her grandfather.

Dragging the packed crate onto the porch, Constable Parker jerked his head over his shoulder toward the front room and said, "I'll bring the missus by tomorrow and she'll clean up them stains, Miz Alexander. Don't you give it another thought."

"You are too kind, sir," she responded. "I'm near exhaustion and I simply don't think I could face that dreadful task today. Plus, I promised Doc Engle that I'd sit with Levi Campbell tomorrow."

Immediately, unexpected doubts assailed Magnolia. Just the chance to speak Levi's name sent Maggie's heart racing. But if one man had betrayed her, would another? Could she ever place her confidence in the word of any other man? She sensed her spirit's very core of trust crumbling. Uncle Cahill's treasonous secrets robbed Maggie of her previous naiveté and left only suspicion and mistrust in its place. Still, a yearning for someone to disprove her cynicism bubbled to the top of her thoughts. She longed for Levi to dispel the blackness now saturating her soul, but the blackness even tainted her longing.

The freshly rooted shame sprouted to produce a malignant weed that began, even now, to eat away at Maggie's soul. Could someone as upstanding as Levi care for a woman raised by a criminal? Immediately, she recalled Preacher Eakin's sermon text from a fortnight ago: "Therefore if any man be in Christ, he is a new creature: old things are passed away; behold, all things are become new." If that verse were true, then Maggie knew she should focus on her status with Christ, not on her family origins. But what she was "supposed" to do somehow got lost in the hurricane of insecurity now attacking her soul.

With her spirit in tumult, Maggie reached for the open door. Originally intending to pull it shut, she stopped with her hand on the loose knob. "Constable, if you don't mind, I'd appreciate your patience for just another minute or two. I think I'd like to say 'good-bye' to this ol' place."

"Of course," he replied respectfully.

Maggie's footsteps on the wooden floors echoed throughout the house as she made her way to the kitchen. At last, she stopped and stared out the window over the drysink.

She had watched her uncle Cahill from this spot on countless mornings as he headed toward the barn to begin his workday. Never again. She would never see her beloved uncle again. But the feelings Maggie expected to flood over her at this life-changing moment of farewells never came. Only numbness claimed her. Numbness, left in the wake of the hurricane of insecurity. There were no tears, no what-might-have-beens, no ache in her soul. . .only the numbness. Feeling as if she were ninety, Magnolia retraced her steps back onto the front porch. The youthful girl from last week seemed to have vanished, and in her place was a weathered woman, ready to embrace death. Without the slightest desire to look back, she climbed into her wagon and followed the constable onto the road, headed for town.

When Maggie and the constable pulled up in front of the boardinghouse, she fully expected Widow Baker to meet her on the porch ready with a tongue-lashing. Instead, Maggie had to go in search of her landlady. The door to the kitchen had been pulled shut, and Maggie recognized the widow's gentle voice as she conversed with another woman. From the tone of the garbled conversation wafting through the closed door, Maggie formed the distinct impression that the woman with the unfamiliar voice was terribly distraught. Not wanting to interrupt, Maggie returned to the stoop alone to assist Constable Parker in carrying the cedar chest and crate up to her room.

With Maggie's things safely deposited in her room, she watched from the front steps as the constable mounted his high-spirited gelding and prepared to lead Maggie's sagging mare and wagon back to the livery stable. Ruff sat in the constable's hay-strewn wagon barking into the humid air as the lawman tipped his hat and took off down the muddy street.

Weary in body and soul, Maggie dragged herself up the stairs to her bedroom. She should do the polite thing and offer Widow Baker her assistance with supper preparations. But the muffled voices floating from the kitchen suggested that Mrs. Baker's attentions weren't focused on supper anyway.

I can't face another person right now—and I certainly don't feel like meeting someone new. Maggie hung a hurriedly scribbled "Sleeping, Please do not disturb" note on the hook outside her door. Without even bothering to pull back her goose-down comforter or remove her shoes, she collapsed across the bed.

❧

The chiming mantel clock in the parlor jarred the fully clothed Maggie from her fitful, dream-filled sleep. One. . . two. . .three times the clock rang. Three o'clock in the morning, yet she didn't even remember lying down. In those fuzzy moments between sleep and consciousness, Maggie struggled to separate reality from her vivid dreams. Was the convalescing knight in shining armor, Levi Campbell, with his sparkling eyes and captivating smile, just a figment of her midnight imagination?

Maybe it's all been a horrible nightmare. Uncle Cahill couldn't have possibly been murdered. He can't really be dead. For a fleeting moment, Maggie convinced herself that only her wildest dreams could conjure up a story so surreal. How preposterous to even dream a tale that turned Uncle Cahill into a stagecoach robber wanted by the law. But as her eyes adjusted to the soft moonlight streaming through her window, her mind accepted the wrenching reality. Real life can be worse than the most awful of apparitions.

The rumble of her stomach reminded Maggie that she hadn't eaten since lunch yesterday. The only sound that greeted her when she opened her bedroom door was the rattled snoring of the rotund peddler, Mr. Winsek, on the third floor. With an outstretched hand, she felt her way through the darkness and down the staircase to the deserted kitchen. Turning up the kerosene lantern, Maggie surveyed the available possibilities that might appease her hunger. Widow Baker had hidden one of her wonderful pound cakes inside the Dutch oven, where mice couldn't and Mr. Winsek *wouldn't* find it. Maggie topped a thick slice with several hand-picked blackberries and gobbled the sweet meal down in a matter of seconds. Her mental list of things to apologize to Widow Baker for which was growing ever longer, but Maggie was certain that the kind-hearted woman would understand.

Lighting another kerosene lantern, she carried it to her room so she didn't have to stumble around in the dark. Accompanied by the smell of burning kerosene, she crossed the room to the cedar chest. The wooden lid creaked softly as she inched it open. Thrusting her hand to the bottom of the chest, she immediately felt the scrolled packet she had hastily hidden at the constable's surprise interruption.

The soft lamplight threw eerie shadows across the "Wanted" poster and cast a sinister aura around the sketch of the man she had always called Uncle Cahill. Holding the paper close, she placed the lantern on the nightstand

and settled onto the bed. Before reading, she studied the pen and ink drawing again, and the inner battle began raging once more.

Is there anyone around me who is who they seem to be? Is there no one in this world I can trust? If someone like this impostor James Calloway could dupe and deceive me for a lifetime, how can I begin to believe a stranger like Levi Campbell? Take care, girl. She warned herself, *Guard your heart. Don't be duped again!*

Maggie held Uncle Cahill's letter and contemplated whether to finish reading it now or wait for a day when she was not so emotionally fragile. At last, she convinced herself to read the letter through to the end. No matter what other shocking revelations she would be forced to face, she decided to meet them head-on. Maggie skimmed her uncle's letter and found the place where she had been interrupted earlier.

Now, before you get the wrong idea, let me hurry and say that I did not mean to harm or kill your family that day. They truly did die when their wagon rolled down an embankment into the Arkansas River. But it weren't no snake that frightened the mules that day. It was me—making my getaway after holding up that stage.

Where do I begin to explain the events that led up to this fateful day? I suppose I could sum up my life prior to that day in just a few brief words. As a Federalist soldier, I was captured by Rebel forces during the battle at Spotsylvania in 1864. They were marching us to a prison, when I was able to make an escape, along with another fella. Being pretty well fed up with war and politics altogether, we decided to head off toward the new frontier and put our past behind us. I didn't have anything to go home to Pennsylvania for, anyway, as my mother had died of the cholera a couple of years earlier and my papa had deserted us both before I was even borned.

Well, I'm sorry to say that I fell into some mighty bad company when I settled in Kansas. Hangin around the saloons and gamblin halls, it weren't difficult to find ways to get into trouble. Even so, I had not ever done nothing really terrible, until one day when I lost all I had to a mangy scoundrel at the poker table. Obliged to either pay my debt or face the killin end of a shootin iron, I was forced into service as what they call a road agent in an express mail heist. Out in the wide-open spaces of the Kansas prairie, it weren't too hard to hold up the mail carriers and stagecoaches in those days, and after I paid off my gamblin debt, I just kept on in that line of work. I never did have to kill nobody, though. Most of those folks I robbed seemed more than happy to turn over money that weren't their own to begin with if it meant breathin for another day.

That terrible morning in May started out as just another workday for me. I landed enough loot in that stage job that I figured I would lay low for a good long while. I even thought about giving up thievin altogether and maybe headin for California.

Well, I had made a clean getaway and was several miles down the trail, but I wanted to put a safe distance between me and the stage I'd just robbed, so I kept on driving my horse as fast as she would go.

Your folkses wagon seemed to spring up from out a nowhere. There was nothin none of us could do to stop their startled mule team before they went headlong off the trail and into the soft sands of the riverbank. By the time I could scramble to the bottom, all of your kin had breathed their last. They had been crushed to death under the weight of the wagon and mule team. I heard you cryin up towards the top of the hill and hurried to find you. You came right to me, throwing your arms around my neck. I knew I couldn't just leave those bodies for the animals or Indians to find. Even a fella as rotten as me couldn't do a thing like that. So I settled you down and started in diggin one big grave in the best spot I could find. I did not have the time to go and fix em each a grave. After that, I started collectin the things that had been scattered about, and I came across that big family Bible and your mama's diary. That evenin as you slept beside me in front of a campfire, I set in a readin your mama's stories. Each page seemed to be written just for me. She told about how Jesus Christ had come into her and your papa's hearts, changin em for the better. She told about how useless and pitiful life had been before they knew God. She didn't see how anyone could face life without Christ.

I read from that Bible and your mama's diary

most of the night. And, the more I read, the more I could see what an awful person I was. How much I needed forgivin. I didn't know if I did it right, but I asked God to forgive me and help me to give up my wicked ways. I decided then an there to turn in the loot from my robbin and take whatever punishment came my way.

I planned to fix up the wagon and carry you with me to turn over to the nearest lawman. That lawman happened to be a fella by the name of Dallas Blankenship. I walked into his jail with you in my arms, piled my money and you on his desk, and said I wanted to turn myself in.

Before I could even say who I was, he offered to strike a deal. He said I could go a free man if I would just leave the money and take you with me. He had no way of handlin a baby in the middle of Kansas and all he cared about was recoverin the money.

I suppose if I'd stopped to think about it awhile, I'd a knowd somethin wasn't right, but I figured it was just God givin me a break. I drove out of town and set beside the Arkansas River for a good long while tryin to figure out what to do next. It just come to me that there weren't nobody that knewed your family was dead. And it wouldn't do anybody no harm if I was to take on the name of your uncle and start a new life somewheres far away. Seein as how I was the one responsible for your folks dyin, I figured God woulda wanted me to take care of you. Well, my sweet little Magnolia, that's how you and I came to settle here and how I took to raisin you.

It weren't til today that I found out that I was still a wanted man. That crooked lawman, Dallas Blankenship, showed up at my door. I'd remember those beady eyes anywhere. He was a wavin this wanted poster under my nose and threatenin to turn me in for the reward if I didn't give him some gold he thought I had. But there ain't no gold. Said he'd give me a day to either get the gold or pay him the cash before he would go to the law. That was just four hours ago, but Maggie, I don't have to think any more. I know what I have to do. He can turn me in to the law, but I can't go back to those connivin old ways. Tomorrow when he shows up, I'll refuse to pay. If he does turn me in, I hope you'll find it in your heart to come and visit me, and let me explain, face to face, the rest of the story that I just couldn't put down on paper. If this Blankenship fella is as crooked as I think he is, tomorrow he may kill me for refusing to give in to his demands. I think he's got more reason to run from the law than I do these days and I don't suppose he's going to run to the constable and turn me in.

The good Lord will see to it that justice is done. Don't take this matter into your own hands, as I know you'll be tempted to do. Show this letter to the constable and let him track down Dallas Blankenship—or whatever name he's usin these days.

Dearest Maggie, I know it was wrong of me not to tell you all this before. I've begged God every day to forgive me for bein dishonest with you. I'm not much of one to give advice, but Maggie, please always remember that I love you dearly, and God loves you, too.

All my love and devotion,
James Calloway,
alias Cahill Alexander.

Maggie let the letter fall to the floor as she fell backward onto the feather pillow, her head throbbing with too many new thoughts and mysteries. While answering many questions, the letter had also posed a new mystery. Who was the ex-lawman who had murdered her uncle? Was he, even now, a part of Dogwood's citizenry? With Uncle Cahill dead and buried in the churchyard, Magnolia didn't know how she would ever discover the man's identity. The very thought of taking the letter and "Wanted" poster to Constable Parker humiliated Maggie beyond measure. She could never face the constable or anyone else in this town if Uncle Cahill's crooked past were known. But was she willing to let his murderer roam free because of her shame?

In a matter of hours, Maggie's foundation of trust in mankind, and in God Himself, had been severely shaken. *Nothing is as it seems to be. No one is who he says he is.* These thoughts played over and over through her mind. Already the night was giving way to the soft light of morning. But Maggie wasn't ready to face a new day.

If Levi Campbell expected her to sit with him today, then he would be sorely disappointed. At once, her former reaction to Levi mocked her. She could no longer allow her heart to be ensnared by a man, even one as charming as he. She had only just met him. How could she be sure he was as upright as he seemed? Even if he were Travis Campbell's brother, that guaranteed nothing. On the other hand, if he were as upright as his older brother was, what could Magnolia, an orphan raised by a common criminal, possibly offer the well-bred cattleman?

five

Maggie bathed and changed into a comfortable cotton gown, then lay absorbed in her thoughts until the familiar rattling of breakfast preparations mingled with the smell of freshly brewed coffee. Expecting to find the Widow Baker alone, Maggie donned her house robe and walked toward the kitchen. She called a raspy, "Good morning," just before opening the creaky door. To her surprise, two female voices echoed, "Good morning."

Next to Widow Baker stood a dark-haired woman cracking eggs into a bowl. The ruddy-cheeked stranger wore one of the widow's favorite silk brocade dressing gowns. Several sizes too small, the elegant fabric stretched across her abdomen to reveal the young lady's impending motherhood.

"Oh, you poor dear," the soft-spoken landlady expressed the oft-repeated sentiment and pulled out a chair from the kitchen table. Deftly, she motioned for Magnolia to take a seat. "You look worn out before the day's even begun. Sit down here and let me fix you a cup of coffee and a plate of these nice eggs."

Widow Baker poured coffee from the steaming pot into her favorite porcelain cup and saucer and handed the warm beverage to Maggie. "You gave me quite a scare yesterday, Miss Alexander," the doting widow said as she overflowed Maggie's coffee cup with the addition of fresh cream. I'm glad to see that you made it home safe and sound."

Relieved that she couldn't find an appropriate place to comment, Magnolia allowed the genteel Mrs. Baker to continue. "I know you must be exhausted. I understand about grieving. Even when you sleep you find no rest.

"Oh my, where are my manners? You two haven't been introduced." Widow Baker turned to the expectant mother. "Magnolia Alexander, I'd like you to meet Miss Louella Simpson. She's going to be staying with us for a while."

Maggie had tried to surreptitiously study the young woman. *Miss, not* Mrs. *Simpson?* She only hoped her overwhelming curiosity wasn't blatantly apparent. "I'm so very pleased to make your acquaintance, Miss Simpson. I know you will be quite happy here at Miz Baker's boardinghouse."

The new tenant cast Maggie a weak and sympathizing smile, revealing yellowed, crooked teeth. "Miz Baker told me about your loss, Miss Alexander. I'm so sorry. I understand your uncle was a wonderful man."

For the first time in her life, Maggie found it impossible to agree with a positive comment about Uncle Cahill. Even though she could not ignore the twist of agony this realization brought to her soul, she chose to not address the statement. Instead, she watched as Widow Baker skillfully dumped the eggs into an iron skillet atop the cooking stove and grappled for a change in subject. With the eggs' telltale fragrance increasing Magnolia's appetite, her muddled mind finally stumbled upon a topic that needed to be addressed.

"Miz Baker, I know this is a great deal to ask of you, but I'm wondering if you would deliver a message to Dr.

Engle's office for me this morning. You see, I agreed to sit with his patient, Levi Campbell, today. But I am simply not up to the task. I believe I am going to spend the entire day in bed, if you don't mind." Wearily, she rubbed her temples.

"Oh, Miss Alexander," Louella interrupted before the widow had a chance to respond, "please allow me to deliver your message for you. I had planned to stop in and speak with Dr. Engle today, anyway."

"Well, all right, then," Maggie agreed. "If you're sure you don't mind. I'll just run upstairs after breakfast and prepare a note. And thank you, Miss Simpson."

"Louella, call me Louella, please."

"I'd be honored if you'd address me as Maggie from now on as well," she replied before nibbling the mountain of scrambled eggs that Widow Baker had set before her.

❧

"Well, it's been quite a number of days since your injury, and I believe it won't be long before you are strong enough to travel out to Travis and Rachel's farm," Dr. Engle announced as he entered Levi's room, rattling a breakfast tray.

Levi turned from the window as the comment hit him like a rock between the eyes. Whatever had possessed him to let Dr. Engle catch him out of bed? Levi knew his brother and sister-in-law were anxious to have him in their home and under their care. And he couldn't impose on the good doctor indefinitely. Still, he wasn't prepared to think about leaving. Desperately, he wondered how he would ever see Magnolia again.

"When do you think I should go?" Levi nonchalantly tossed the question toward Dr. Engle, his voice disguising the turmoil raging within.

Levi had wrestled with sleep most of the night, but he couldn't blame his restlessness on physical discomfort. Rather, his insomnia was due to the anticipation of Magnolia's arrival and the fleeting, few hours he would spend in her care. As the circumstances appeared, those hours would be a precious few, indeed.

"There's no hurry, but when Miss Alexander comes in this morning, I'll ride out to Travis's and see what day works out best for him. Maybe you can go as early as tomorrow or the next day if you're up to the trip. I need to check on Rachel, anyway. I wasn't happy about her coloring the last time she was in. She looks mighty peaked."

Levi hoped Travis didn't hurry to rescue him. This was one time Levi didn't want his big brother rushing to his aid! Levi's irrational resentment toward his older brother boiled to the surface as he frowned toward the red-doored saloon across the street.

All of his life, Levi had been hounded by comments like, "Why can't you be more like your brother?" "Your brother would never do such a thing!" "Aren't you Travis Campbell's kid brother?"

But Levi wanted to just be himself. When their father insisted that Levi attend the same Boston law school where Travis studied, Levi adamantly refused. He wasn't meant to be a lawyer. His home was the range. So he had taken his poetry and his stallion and spent his days with the livestock.

Travis had never really done anything to deserve Levi's rancor, and Levi was beginning to feel like a cad because of these negative feelings. Something insisted the time had come to grow up and put this childhood pettiness behind him.

His older brother had never been more than a gracious help, were Levi to ask his assistance. And he could certainly use Travis's advice in regard to Miss Magnolia Alexander. Before Travis married Rachel, he had his choice of El Paso's maidens. Levi, on the other hand, rarely enjoyed the company of one from the female persuasion, unless he counted female cows. Now, Levi found himself blundering through the beginnings of a relationship with Magnolia Alexander. Hopefully, his lack of skill in dealing with ladies would in no way push her away.

Oh, Lord, give me wisdom in my interactings with Miss Alexander. And. . .and help me with this absurd jealousy, Levi prayed silently. *I know I should be thankful to have a brother like Travis. I reckon the reason I've been so irked is because I figure I can never measure up to him. That's probably not fair to him or me. Still, Lord, if you could work it out that I could find a woman like. . .like Magnolia Alexander to fall in love with, I'd never need to be jealous of Travis again.*

Levi sealed his silent bargain with an "amen" and absently watched the saloon's swinging red door open and close with the arrival and exit of patrons. *It's mighty early to be drinking,* Levi thought as he caught sight of a scroungy pair rushing onto the boardwalk.

The grimy men wore tattered, filthy clothes and shapeless hats. The pair, both clutching whiskey bottles, untied the reins of their horses, tethered at the hitching post. In one fluid motion, they mounted their steeds and spurred them into a full gallop. The resulting jolt sent one man's hat toppling to the side, and he grappled to retrieve it as a cascade of matted red hair spilled forth. *A woman! One of the men was really a woman! A woman with hair the same color as that bandit who had shot him.* At once, Levi's knees buckled as though they were made of jelly. "She's the one," he muttered. He would have recognized the frizzled red hair in a crowd of a thousand.

"Doc, I. . ."

Dr. Engle immediately stepped toward Levi, guiding him to the bed. "Boy, you look like you've seen a ghost. You'd better lie down. I was afraid you were overdoing it. Maybe I was a bit hasty in assuming you were ready to leave—"

"No, Doc. You don't understand. It's one of those lady bandits—riding with that fella down the street."

By the time the doctor crossed the room and looked out the expansive window, Levi strained to see any sign that the two had been in the muddy street.

"I'll see if I can stir up the constable." The physician jumped into action. "I hate to leave you, but I don't see that I have any other choice since Maggie hasn't arrived yet. Now, get yourself back to bed. I'll hurry back as soon as I can."

Levi sank onto the pillow and eyed his breakfast tray sitting on the nearby table. As the outer door closed behind Dr. Engle, Levi's sense of helplessness particularly frustrated him. He was accustomed to handling whatever situation might come, no matter how challenging or difficult. But Levi was quickly learning that a gunshot wound had a way of turning a capable man into a weakling.

What would he do if someone intent on doing him harm were to enter after seeing the doctor leave? Levi was certainly in no condition to stand and fight, and he had given

Travis his Peacemaker for safekeeping.

"A cowboy can do without a lot of things in life, but he should never be caught without his gun!" his papa used to always say. And those words proved true more than once out on the range. Why had he not remembered Papa's constant admonition? He should have kept his gun with him.

His stomach growled, and Levi sat up with plans to settle in the chair near the table holding those mellow-scented strips of bacon that now tormented his appetite. But all hunger vanished as the front door banged shut and an unfamiliar, feminine voice called out, "Hal-low, is anyone here?" He had hoped the slamming door would signal the arrival of Magnolia Alexander. But Levi had heard the gentle lilt of Magnolia's musical tongue enough to know that the woman calling out was not his angelic nurse. The mystery intruder's being a woman did little to dissuade the apprehension overwhelming Levi. He tried to tell himself that his fears were irrational. But his stomach clenched at the memory of that redheaded bandit he had just seen.

You coward! Afraid of a woman. Despite his mental castigation, he noticed the iron bar propped beside the cold fireplace and stood to retrieve it.

"Oh, hello. I wasn't sure if anyone was around." The feminine voice took on the face of a woman with blotched skin and dark, plaited hair. Her eyes guileless, she peered at him from around the door. "I do hope I didn't disturb you. I'm searchin' for the doctor. Is he in?"

Levi sighed with relief and settled back onto the bed as the woman stepped through the doorway. Obviously heavy with child, she seemed as harmless as Levi's grandmother.

"No, he had to step out for a short while. I'm not any

help as far as doctoring is concerned. But I'd be more than happy to pass along a message."

"W–Well," the unidentified visitor stammered with reluctance, "I. . .I did need to see him about a p–personal matter, though it's nothing urgent. Nothing that can't wait. Then, I also promised to deliver a note of explanation for Dr. Engle from his nurse, Magnolia Alexander. I suppose she wouldn't mind if you gave it to him instead. She's not going to be able to come to work today."

Levi took the perfumed note from the stranger's extended hand and stared at the envelope with downcast eyes, hoping to mask his profound disappointment.

Magnolia's not coming today. Magnolia's not coming today. Magnolia's not coming today. The words began a melancholic chorus in his mind, which seemed to dim the sunshine pouring through the window. Levi held the sealed letter under his nose and breathed deeply of Magnolia's lavender perfume. He longed to touch the hands that likewise bore this fragrance. Magnolia's hands. Did she suspect the power she slowly gained over him? For hours, his thoughts had dwelled on nothing else but being in her presence once more. *She's not coming. Was it something I did or said?*

The temptation to tear open the envelope and read Magnolia's note to Dr. Engle was almost more than Levi could bear. The impropriety of such an act would be inexcusable. Still, he felt he had a right to know why she wasn't keeping her word. Magnolia's expressive face certainly bore witness to the fact that she felt the same overwhelming tug of attraction now drawing Levi to her. If she were holding back on her emotions, he understood. She had just suffered a terrible loss. Furthermore, she was a gentlewoman with a lady's sense of propriety. Certainly, Magnolia's absence today represented more than truancy from work. She was avoiding him, or his name wasn't Levi Jacob Campbell.

As the expectant mother stirred, Levi realized he had forgotten her very presence. "I guess I should be going now," she said as she backed away.

"Please, wait," Levi called before she stepped across the door's threshold. "I'm wondering if you could be so kind as to deliver a return message to Miss Alexander for me."

"Why, certainly," the woman replied as she hovered near the doorway.

I'm not going to make it easy for you to brush me off, Magnolia. Levi frantically racked his brain for the appropriate words as he reached for paper and pen on the nearby nightstand. Choking down a grimace, he painfully grasped the pen in his right hand, extending from the sling. In a barely legible script, he scribbled, "Be an *angel* and come back as soon as you can. I'm anxious to hear you read *Huckleberry Finn.*" Upon her last visit, Magnolia had placed a book on the nightstand—a book she never read due to their lengthy conversation. Upon perusal, Levi discovered the book to be penned by one of his favorite authors, Mark Twain. Even though he had read *Huck Finn* at least three times, Levi longed to hear Magnolia's musical voice pose the words on his ear.

Folding the paper over once and once again, he passed it to the waiting woman and said, "Thank you, ma'am. I really appreciate your kindness in delivering this message for me. I do hope Miss Alexander is well."

"I'll see that she gets it first thing after she wakes up. And I'll tell her of your concern. I'm sure she's going to be just fine. I have a feelin' she's just tuckered out; that's all. Now, if you'll excuse me, sir. . ." The meek messenger turned and hurried out the door.

❧

When Dr. Engle clamored back in the door a short while later, Levi had finished his breakfast and turned his mind solely to the unread contents of Magnolia's note. However, Dr. Engle, whirling with the thrill of the chase, bounded to Levi's bedside, his eyes sparkling with excitement.

"I found the constable." The doctor set straight his twisted coat collar and removed the bowler from atop his well-greased hair. "He took off, hot on her trail, as soon as I told him about your sighting of that redheaded bandit and her male sidekick. I tell you, Levi, I think he's got a good chance of catching them, thanks to our quick work. I wonder just what they are up to, sneaking around town. If we're lucky, they'll lead the constable to the other female rascal as well."

"Great!"

"Say, are you feeling any better?" he asked, scrutinizing Levi. "I'm surprised Maggie's not here yet."

Levi held up the sealed note. "She sent this. Evidently, she's not coming in today. Her messenger said the note would explain," he said, trying to hide his raging curiosity.

Gazing at the envelope, Dr. Engle drew his brows into a puzzled frown. "Did the Widow Baker bring this by?" he asked, a thinly veiled note of expectation in his voice.

"Well, I haven't met a Widow Baker, and this lady didn't give out her name, but she was about twenty years old and

I'd guess about eight months along in the motherly way. Said she needed to speak with you about a personal matter as well, so she'll be back."

"No, that's definitely not Sarah Baker." The doctor's ironic smile held a twist of mystery. "Oh, well, let's see what Maggie has to say. If it's all right with you, I'll just read it aloud." Dr. Engle's impish remarks suggested Levi's interest in the nurse's letter had not gone unnoticed.

"Whatever you prefer," Levi replied coolly, inwardly scolding himself for being too transparent.

Dr. Engle positioned his spectacles on his nose and, ignoring Levi's counterfeit indifference, began reading what she wrote.

My Dear Dr. Engle,

I do sincerely hope and pray that my absence today does not present too grave a hardship on you or Mr. Campbell. I had every intention of honoring my commitment when I left there yesterday. However, I now find myself weary to the point of exhaustion. Let me try to explain. When I departed your company in the morning, I set out for Uncle Cahill's farm in order to prepare the house for a new owner. I fear that I attempted to undertake more than I was capable of at this time of deep sorrow. For as I set about the task of sorting through my uncle's things, grievous emotion overwhelmed me. Now I feel that the best remedy is a day in bed. I believe I know you well enough to ascertain that this is also what you would prescribe. I am confident that I will be up and about by this time tomorrow and I shall greet you in your office then.

Please extend my regrets to Mr. Campbell and convey my promise to begin reading from Twain's "Huck Finn" when I return.

Yours most sincerely,
Magnolia Alexander

"Well, there you have it, Levi. She'll be back on the job first thing tomorrow. I know Miss Alexander. She's not one to let life's troubles get the best of her."

Unconvinced that Magnolia's actions were not meant as a snub, Levi tried to analyze the words he had just heard. *Her note seems entirely too stilted to me. What is it that she's left unsaid?* He would just have to wait until she walked into his room tomorrow to know for certain if his fears were false or confirmed. One look at her candid countenance would answer Levi's dilemma. In the meantime, he would double his efforts to win her heart. *I'll replace your uncle Cahill as the man you can depend on, Magnolia. Just you wait and see.*

As Levi pondered what new approach he would take to solicit the affections of his charming nurse, the doctor's outer office door flew open again. He started and wondered what it took for an ailing fella to get any peace. But his complaints stopped short of vocalization when he recognized his brother's voice. "Doc. Dr. Engle. Are you here?"

"Yes. Yes, in here," the doctor replied, quickly shoving Maggie's note into his coat pocket as he turned to leave the room. Before Dr. Engle could manage to close Levi's bedroom door behind him, Travis Campbell had bounded across the hardwood floor and grabbed the doctor's shoulders in his muscular hands. Without so much as a glance at his brother, Travis launched into a frantic plea.

"Sir, please." The elder Campbell tugged at Dr. Engle's sleeves, practically dragging the physician from the room. "You've got to come to our place. And hurry. There's something terribly wrong with Rachel. She's in dreadful pain." Agony seemed to ooze from Travis's eyes. "I think the baby's trying to arrive. I told Rachel I'd come for you and get back to her as soon as I could." The frenzied husband implored his skilled friend to follow him as he rushed out the door. "Doc, can you? Won't you? You must come!"

Dr. Engle grabbed his black leather bag from the wall peg and hastily prepared to follow the already departed Travis. Halfway over the threshold, he called out to Levi, "I'll be back as soon as I can. Just do your best to manage things around here."

The jealousy that had plagued Levi earlier now haunted him. *Oh, Lord. You know I would never wish harm or ill on Travis or his family. Please, dear God, help them now! And forgive me, Lord. Forgive me. Help me to relinquish these feelings of inadequacy to you.*

six

Throughout the morning Maggie tried in vain to sleep. The more she pursued relaxation, the more her fretfulness grew. "Idle hands are the devil's workshop," Maggie could still hear her uncle Cahill say. She wasn't accustomed to the life of leisure some championed, and she was beginning to doubt its merit. Magnolia found that, in the absence of productivity, her mind filled with dark thoughts, bitterness, and rage.

In an attempt to blot out the sun streaming through the window, she covered her head with the pillow. As the smells of Mrs. Baker's rose-scented sheets enveloped her, she desperately wanted to mourn her uncle's death by remembering all the good about him. During the wee hours of the night, she had determined that she could never think of him as James Calloway. To her, he would always be Uncle Cahill, regardless of his legal name. But thoughts of his twenty-year deception stubbornly replaced her wonderful memories. Even when her mind turned to Levi, rather than fantasizing about any wonderful possibilities, Maggie wondered if she could ever trust him—or any other man—*ever*. After all, the one man in this world she had completely believed in, in the end, had proven himself untrustworthy.

By midday, the early summer sun had sufficiently heated her room to such a degree that perspiration dampened her hair. *I've got to get out and make myself useful somewhere.* With hands skilled through years of experience, she captured her rebellious hair, now frizzled around the hairline, into its usual chignon. After pouring cool water from the dressing table's porcelain pitcher into a matching bowl, she splashed her face. Chagrined at her reflection in the gilded mirror over the bowl, she stood pinching her cheeks, hoping to give them color. Yet even her most meticulous grooming tricks failed to mask the dark circles underscoring swollen, bloodshot eyes.

She removed the light cotton gown she had donned in the morning's wee hours and put on one of the two mourning dresses the Widow Baker had so thoughtfully lent her. Smoothing the stiff skirt, Maggie reached for her bedroom door's white enameled knob. Just then, she caught sight of a sloppily folded piece of paper that had been shoved under her door. Magnolia picked up the note and shook it open with a quick jerk. *This looks like it was written by a child.* Her eyes darted to the bottom of the page in search of an identifying signature. Finding the note unsigned, she focused her attentions on the brief message.

"Be an *angel* and come back as soon as you can. I'm anxious to hear you read *Huckleberry Finn.*"

Levi Campbell. The note came from Levi, not from a child. She winced as she considered the obvious pain Levi had endured to pen this simple message. Maggie chuckled to herself as she reread Levi's thinly veiled reference to their first verbal exchange. But a sense of foreboding scurried behind the chuckle. Obviously, Levi wasn't the type to let their new relationship die simply because

Magnolia chose to distance herself. Perplexed with her dilemma, Magnolia frowned, refolded the note, crossed the room, and opened her mother's Bible on the bedside table. Tenderly, she tucked Levi's message inside, then hesitated. Sternly pressing her lips together, she removed the note and dropped it into the nearby wastebasket. Her spine stiff, she retraced her steps and left the room.

Tiptoeing noiselessly down the stairs, her traitorous heart beat with regret over discarding Levi's note. Would Levi think her heartless? He must have been terribly disappointed by her absence to have written a note despite the pain it caused him.

But before she reached the kitchen door, Maggie's common sense had once more overruled her heart. She simply could not allow herself to trust any man, not even one as sweet-talking as Levi Campbell. Stubbornly, she decided she would show no more concern over disappointing him. Furthermore, if he learned the truth about her upbringing, Levi might very easily decide Magnolia was not the breed of woman that would interest him.

"Hello," Louella Simpson greeted Maggie as she came through the swinging kitchen door. "I was just fixin' to make us a lunch tray," she said, pointing toward a wooden tray laden with two glasses of lemonade. "I didn't expect that you'd leave your bed today, and I figured the two of us could share the noon meal in your room. That is. . .if you didn't mind," she said uncertainly. But before Maggie had a chance to answer, Louella rushed on, "Oh, before I forget it, I slid a note under your door. Did you notice it?" Her speculative gaze suggested Louella had already conjured a number of scenarios regarding the handsome patient.

"Yes, I found it," Maggie said, purposefully walking toward the loaf of thick-crusted bread on the kitchen counter. "Thank you for all the trouble you've gone to for me today." With a stained butcher knife, she cut a wide slice of the bread and doggedly changed the subject.

"You needn't bother with a lunch tray, Louella. You really are too kind. My room is so sweltering it's impossible to rest. And this heat has robbed me of much of an appetite, especially after eating the huge breakfast that you and Mrs. Baker prepared. Can you imagine what August will be like if June is this hot? Anyway, I'll just munch on this bread and a piece of cheese." She removed the glass dome, which rested atop a wooden cheese plate and helped herself to a wedge of mellow cheese. "I thought I might as well see if I could be of some assistance to Widow Baker. Is she around?" Maggie looked through the kitchen's screen door and scanned the backyard, expecting to see Sarah Baker hanging clothes on the line.

"Miz Baker had to do some shopping at the general store, so I offered to help her by peelin' the potatoes for tonight's soup. I've just finished the job and it's hotter than blazes in here. Why don't we both take a glass of lemonade out to the back porch and sit a spell?"

"I'd like that, Louella. Let's do. It will give me a chance to get acquainted with you." Magnolia pulled open a nearby drawer and retrieved one of Mrs. Baker's red checked napkins.

" 'Tisn't likely that I'm the kind of folk you'd want to get to know." Her eyes downcast, Louella gazed forlornly at her thick waistline. She picked up the two tall glasses of freshly poured lemonade and started toward the screen door leading to the back porch.

Maggie set the bread and cheese atop the napkin and insisted on relieving Louella of one of the glasses. At once, Magnolia felt a certain kinship with the bereft young woman. She identified all too well with the hopelessness clouding Louella's eyes. The insecurity. The worries that no one would accept her when they found out the bitter truth. After reading her uncle's note, Magnolia had experienced every one of those emotions. By no means was she carrying an illegitimate child, but she did bear an illegitimate past. A past based on lies. The lies of an outlaw.

"Please don't feel that way for one minute," Magnolia said, sipping the tart, cool lemonade as she paused between the slat-backed rockers. "You've been nothing but helpful, sweet, and kind to me all day." She held one of the chairs steady so Louella could slowly ease herself into it. A gentle breeze rustled the leaves of the oak tree that shaded the east end of the covered porch and both women breathed deeply of the markedly cooler air. Louella pushed her rocker into motion and Maggie soon matched her rhythm. As they tapped out a syncopated cadence on the gray slat floor, Maggie gazed intently into Louella's hazel eyes. Louella's eyes were obviously her best feature.

"If you'd allow me the chance, Louella, I think we could become good friends." Maggie pinched off a bite of bread and cheese and nibbled them.

"But, Miss Maggie, you obviously don't understand. I'm not the kind of woman that a lady of class such as yourself would associate with."

"I wouldn't be much of a lady at all if I looked down my nose at you," Maggie insisted, dusting the bread crumbs from her lap. "Whatever problems you're facing right now, given time and the Lord's help, they will all work out."

Louella began to blink rapidly as she fought back tears. Once again she eyed her protruding abdomen. "My life is such a mess, Miss Maggie. I don't think there's any fixin' it now."

Magnolia's nursing instincts took over as she sympathetically patted the back of Louella's hand. "Sometimes it helps just to share your burdens with another. Why don't you tell me all about it? Perhaps you could start by telling me where you call home. I know you're not from around Dogwood. I'm acquainted with pretty near all the folks in these parts."

"No, I'm not from around here," Louella offered. "I grew up in Pine Bend. Pine Bend, Arkansas, that is. My paw and maw raised chickens and farmed a little land about five miles west of town. My folks, they were good Christians, even though we couldn't make it into church but every now and again. I was reared on the Good Book and my life was pretty normal back then."

Louella's eyes took on a faraway glaze as though she had transported herself back to happier times. Shaking her head slowly from side to side, she started in with her story once again.

"But, a couple years ago, my paw took sick and died. Poor Maw grieved so hard I thought I might lose her, too. That's why I know a little about the sufferin' you're goin' through." Maggie only nodded her head in agreement as Louella spoke.

"After Paw died, Maw and me, we didn't know how we

would manage with the farm and all. But, somehow, we struggled through. One day, though, about this time last year, a smooth talkin', good lookin' Yankee by the name of Silas Turner showed up at our door. He was peddlin' some kind of elixir, swearin' it would cure whatever ailed you. Well, Miss Maggie, just starin' at Mr. Turner cured what ailed *me*! I had been so busy on the farm, I hadn't had time to bother with courtin' any beaus. Besides, the good Lord didn't bless me with an abundance of beauty and I never had any boys bangin' down my door. But this Mr. Turner, he was somethin' different. He showed me attention like no fella had ever done before. He made me feel really and truly purdy for the first time in my life."

Just like Levi makes me feel. Maggie couldn't stop the words from invading her mind.

"Miss Maggie, lookin' back on it now, I realize that Mr. Turner was slicker than snake oil. He said so many sweet things to me, makin' me feel like I was the most beautiful thing he had ever seen. He told me he was goin' to look for work so he could stay close by me. One thing led to another and, before summer's end, I was for sure that he was the man of my dreams and the answer to my prayers.

"My maw tried to tell me that I was rushin' into things and it was all movin' too far, too soon, but I wouldn't listen. I was just sure that Silas Turner and me were meant for one another. It was the first time in my life that I can remember being at real odds with my maw. From that first feud with Maw on, I avoided her, and she steered clear of me. I figured I'd best just keep quiet and let time prove that I was right."

Louella rubbed her eyes, heavy with dark circles.

"Things happened quick between Mr. Turner and me. I wasn't used to bein' fawned over and adored. He treated me like a queen, singin' me songs and bringin' me flowers. When he first kissed me, I found myself wantin' more, but I did the respectable thing and pushed him away.

"But one day, when Maw was gone to a quiltin' bee, Silas and I were out doin' chores in the barn and he started sayin' such sweet words to me. He kissed me again. Only this time, I kissed him back. I'd never felt such wonderful feelin's in all my born days. I figured that we were goin' to be married soon, the way he was talkin' and all, and I wanted him to be happy, too. I didn't see how somethin' that felt so good could be all that sinful and bad. I am ashamed to say it now, Miss Maggie, but since I thought we were goin' to be husband and wife quick enough, I just let Silas do whatever he wanted to that day.

"After that day in the barn, it was next to impossible to tell Silas 'no'. He looked for more and more chances for us to be alone together. Each time, I'd try pushin' him to set a weddin' date, and he always hedged. Finally after 'bout three weeks of that, I told him we *had* to get married or all of it was gonna stop.

"The next afternoon, I waited on the porch for Silas to show up for supper as we'd planned, but he never came. I went into town lookin' for him the following mornin' and the hotel clerk said he had checked out and said that he was headin' west. It was all I could do to keep from bustin' into tears right there in the hotel lobby, but I saved my tears for the journey home.

"With the trouble between Maw and me, I wasn't about

to admit that she had been right all along. I didn't want to 'fess up to lettin' him love me the way only a husband should love a wife. I don't think I coulda ever looked my maw in the eyes again. I never felt so all alone as I did that day."

I know all about consuming loneliness and secrets too terrible to share with another living soul, Maggie thought as Louella took a long drink of her lemonade. *But maybe someday I'll be able to share with someone in the same way Louella is sharing with me.* Levi's face flashed through Maggie's mind. Would she ever dare to reveal her true self and deepest secrets to him? A desperate longing for such a relationship swept over Maggie and new tears stung her eyes. But what if Levi was nothing but another smooth-talker like Louella's Silas Turner? Could she be sure she could trust him? Too choked with emotion to even speak, Maggie deposited her uneaten bread and cheese on the nearby table as Louella continued.

The expectant mother brushed aside her own silent tears. "The only thing I could think to do was to run away from home. I think I was hopin' to find Silas and convince him to take me with him. So, when Maw was in the vegetable garden picking beans, I took what money she had stashed in her hatbox, left her a note tellin' her good-bye, and snuck off into the woods.

"Even though I was already plumb worn out from cryin', I walked all that afternoon and through the night. The next day, I was lucky enough to catch a westbound stage that had stopped off in some little Arkansas town. By the time the stage driver stopped to water his horses in Dogwood, I'd just about given up all hope of running into

Silas and I figured that, even if I did, I couldn't convince him to come back with me. It was then that I saw a "Help wanted" sign in the window of the Dogwood saloon.

"Dogwood looked pretty good to me right about then." She rubbed a thin film of perspiration from her upper lip and sipped her lemonade. "I was so tired. I just didn't feel like I could go another mile. Before the stage left town, I was standin' behind the saloon counter pourin' whiskey for the local men.

"Now, I knew it wasn't respectable work for a Christian girl to do, but I figured I had already fallen below my station by what I'd done with Silas Turner and I didn't deserve any better. I reckon I wasn't thinkin' too highly of myself right then." Louella threw a shy grin to Maggie.

"And you've been in Dogwood ever since?" Maggie asked.

"Yes. Mr. Wentworth, who was managin' the saloon for Sweeney back then, put me up in a room over the bar and I hardly ever left the place," Louella replied. "In fact, I stayed behind that counter as much as I could. You see, after a bit of time passed, I realized the full consequences of what Mr. Turner and I had done when we were alone." Louella's hand dropped to her stomach and no further words needed to be said.

Maggie sadly shook her head.

"That explains why I've not seen you before. I don't think I've even looked inside the doors of a saloon. Uncle Cahill used to tell me that a saloon was nothing but a den of iniquity and I should stay as far away as I possibly could." As the words left her mouth, Maggie pondered the irony of her uncle's wisdom. Undoubtedly, he had learned that truth by firsthand experience.

"Your uncle must've been a pretty wise man, Miss Maggie. There weren't much that went on in there that was any good. But I'd probably still be there today if Jed Sweeney hadn't showed up to check up on Mr. Wentworth and his saloon last week. Sweeney took one look at me and sent both me and Wentworth packin'—and without our due pay. He said Wentworth might have been soft, but he sure wasn't gonna be. Said he didn't need any liabilities like a barmaid in the "family way" workin' in his saloon. That Mr. Sweeney had me so frightened and flustered that I just grabbed what I could carry of my things and I skedaddled from there.

"You know, Miss Maggie, I should be glad Sweeney gave me the boot. I don't think I could bring myself to work too long for that man."

Louella's words sent the image of Jed Sweeney flashing across Maggie's mind. His inky eyes. His thin frame. His offer to buy Uncle Cahill's ranch. Should Magnolia sell the estate to a man who would throw out Louella without hesitation?

"So how did you happen to end up here?" Maggie asked.

"Well, when I left the saloon, I didn't know where to go. I wandered through town until I found myself sittin' in Dotty's Café with my head between my hands. I guess I was cryin', I don't really remember, but I musta looked a sight, 'cause Miz Baker stopped to ask if there was anything she could do to help me. I tell you, Miz Baker's been nothin' but wonderful to me ever since. When she found out that I had no place to sleep and no money to pay, she took me in and said she'd give me free room and board in exchange for help around the house."

The two women sat in silence for several long moments as Maggie pondered the overabundance of life's heartaches. She patted Louella's hand once again as she softly asked, "What are your plans for when the baby comes?"

Louella shrugged and sighed deeply. "I haven't wanted to think about it much, but I know I need to sort it out soon. I don't mind tellin' you, Miss Maggie, I'm plumb scared. Miz Baker said I really ought to be checked over by the doctor, and I intended on talkin' with Doc Engle when I delivered your note today. But he was out, so I guess I'll have to try again."

"He was out?" Maggie abruptly stood from her chair. "Dr. Engle was out? Why? Where did he go? Who's caring for Levi Campbell?" The questions tumbled from her lips faster than Louella could respond to a single one.

Louella stammered as she struggled to climb out of her chair. "Well I. . .I don't rightly know. I. . .I assumed that the bedridden fella had addressed these things in his note."

"I think I might be able to answer at least one or two of your questions," Sarah Baker interjected as she opened the screen door and stepped out of the kitchen. With short, precise jerks, she removed her white gloves and held them in a blue-veined hand.

"It appears that Dr. Engle's been called out for an emergency at the Campbell place. I happened to run into Rachel's cousin, Angela Isaacs, outside the store. She said she'd just met Travis running into Dr. Engle's office and that he beseeched her to pray for Rachel. He came tearing out of the doctor's office a few seconds later, jumped on his horse, then galloped off toward his farm. Dr. Engle came out right behind him, carrying his black bag. I hope and pray Rachel's not having troubles with her unborn child."

Maggie grasped her throat, feeling as though she had been thrown into yet another perplexing predicament. Clearly, her duties as a nurse rested with caring for Dr. Engle's patients. Part of her insisted she rush to her medical responsibility. Yet another side of her, the wary side, bade her to avoid Levi Campbell at all costs. Her professional obligations finally overrode her emotions and she muttered, "I. . .I really must go check on the injured Mr. Campbell."

"Have you heard?" Widow Baker answered, her eyes snapping with interest in all the latest stories. "Your patient spotted one of those women bandits with some man coming out of the saloon. Constable Parker is scouring the countryside for them now."

"No. I didn't know that either, but thank the good Lord. I hope Constable nabs 'em. Now, if you'll excuse me," she continued. Maggie spun into action. She raced to her room to retrieve her reticule, gloves, and parasol. Then she hurried past Widow Baker and Louella at the base of the stairs. Stunned, they silently watched Magnolia rush through the front screen door. "I won't be home for supper," she yelled over her shoulder as the screen door slammed behind her.

Hastening from the porch steps and along the rutted road to Dr. Engle's, Magnolia firmly resolved to remain aloof and inexpressive in her dealings with Levi Campbell. *You are going to stay with him out of duty. Nothing more,* Maggie repeatedly admonished herself, refusing even the slightest flutter of excitement. Yet she betrayed her own covenant within seconds of stepping into Levi's room.

seven

Magnolia left her gloves, parasol, and reticule in the front office and entered Levi's room as nonchalantly as her pounding pulse would allow. Despite all her mental vows on Dogwood's Main Street, her heart insisted on palpitating at the sight of Levi Campbell. She had caught him in the act of sitting upright, intently reading the Word of God, like a man in near-perfect health. His attempts to scramble into a reclining position left Magnolia stifling a smile.

"Hello. I hoped you'd come." Levi reached for her hand, his emerald eyes dancing with anticipation.

As if her instincts were bent on betraying her, Magnolia found herself extending her hand toward his, expecting the feel of his callused fingers as they closed around hers, reveling in the warm affection Levi so freely offered. However, a dark cloud of misgiving descended upon her soul, and Magnolia jerked her hand to her side. She balled her fist into a tight knot, firmly set her lips, and turned to the pile of soiled linens stacked in the corner. She didn't dare look at him. She didn't dare ponder the smoldering passion so blatant in his eyes. She didn't dare hope that a man like Levi would continue in his warm regard upon learning the truth of her upbringing.

Once more, the passage from Preacher Eakin's message several weeks past abruptly interrupted her thoughts:

Therefore if any man be in Christ, he is a new creature: old things are passed away; behold, all things are become new. This time, the Bible verse seemed to breathe a wisp of hope upon Magnolia's soul, a hope that was short-lived. For even if she embraced the verse as truth, that did not mean Levi Campbell or anyone else would.

Magnolia pondered the plight of Louella Simpson. She weighed the reaction of most of Dogwood once they learned she was giving birth to an illegitimate child. Regardless of Louella's repentance, regardless of her worth in Christ, Maggie knew that most of the township, most of the church, would scorn her.

Likewise, Maggie's situation would evoke disdain from those who discovered the truth. The hard facts of human nature left Magnolia feeling as if she were sinking into the depths of a dank and dreary pit of despair.

Levi awkwardly cleared his throat.

Refusing to look at him, Magnolia picked up the soiled linens. Loaded with the laundry, she stiffened as his contrite words seemed bent on melting the barriers of her heart.

"Have I. . .in some way offended you, Magnolia?" he asked softly.

She bit her lip as tears of bitterness stung her eyes. *No,* she wanted to yell. *No. You have done nothing. Only Uncle Cahill, the man I thought I could trust. Now I don't know if I can trust a soul. Now I don't know if anyone will even want to associate with me.*

Instead, she hunched her shoulders, muttered a quick "No," and rushed toward the door without a backward glance. In an effort to regain composure, Magnolia occupied her time with household chores and early supper preparations. Levi was visibly gaining strength and no longer needed constant care. However, she could not indefinitely avoid him. Her professional obligations insisted she prepare the patient an evening meal. Desperately trying to harden her heart, Magnolia took a shaking breath before entering his room, holding the tray filled with ham and beans and cornbread.

However, this time her patient no longer claimed the bed. Instead, he sat in the armchair by the opened window and had somehow managed to change from the nightshirt into the stiff jeans and denim shirt that Dr. Engle had provided from the general store. At the sight of Levi's freshly shaven face, Magnolia glanced toward the bowl and pitcher stand to see signs of lather and water.

"I feel like an invalid lying in that bed all day," Levi answered Magnolia's unspoken question.

"It's good to see you gaining some strength." With an air of cool indifference, she refused to meet his gaze. However, the fact that Levi could actually dress himself and sit in the chair suggested that Dr. Engle would soon be releasing his patient. The very idea left Magnolia spinning in disappointment—a disappointment she squelched. As she bent to situate the tray on the nearby table, Maggie felt Levi studying her. At this close proximity, she smelled the lye soap he had used for shaving. Lye soap, and the odor of starch on new garments. Once again, her pulse insisted upon its telltale fluttering, and she determined to remove herself from his presence as soon as her professionalism allowed.

Setting her face like a stern spinster, Magnolia handed

him his fork and desperately tried not to look into his eyes. But despite her valiant attempts to avoid peering into his soul, her gaze slowly traveled from the fork, to his arm in the white sling, past the buttons of the denim shirt, across his thin lips and aristocratic nose, and at last met his questioning scrutiny. The faint attraction that Magnolia initially felt for Levi had gradually grown into the fires of longing. Longing, which his own tormented eyes revealed. Only the lazy, summer sounds of an east Texas town broke the wordless communication that flashed between them—neither could hide the reciprocal fascination.

At once, Levi's earlier inquiry seemed to bounce between them, demanding an answer. *Have I. . .in some way offended you, Magnolia?* The question posed itself so strongly in Maggie's mind that she found herself ready to answer once more.

"Magnolia?" he whispered, again reaching for her hand.

Nervously, she pushed the fork into his opened hand and rushed from his presence. Her own vacillating emotions forced her to exercise a firm self-control of mind over emotions. She could no longer predict what she might feel or what words might spill from her lips. The task of stifling her feelings for Levi was the most difficult assignment she had ever attempted, and it grew more and more impossible as the hours passed.

Like a woman obsessed, Magnolia attacked the dirty dishes stacked on the kitchen counter. In a matter of minutes, she had washed and dried all but one plate. With the evening shadows lengthening, she furiously rubbed the last plate with a cup towel. Whether she wanted to or not,

Magnolia sensed Levi's magnetic presence as if his very spirit were draping itself around her shoulders. No chore, regardless of how frenzied, could blot out Levi. His endearing smile. His open admiration. His obvious devotion to the Lord. In short, Levi Campbell was everything Magnolia would want in a husband. A tremble of yearning rippled through her.

The gentle tinkling of Levi's bedside bell sent a shock of dread through Magnolia. Dread and anticipation. She shouldn't enjoy every second she spent with him, regardless of her yearning. She shouldn't. . .for their potential relationship represented nothing but an impasse. An impasse weighted with heartache. The bell sounded again, and Magnolia set the plate in its spot in the cabinet and walked toward the room. Pausing on the threshold, she raised her brows in silent query.

From his spot by the window, Levi studied her, a spark of mischief in his eyes. "You never read *Huck Finn* to me," he said, lifting the book from his lap.

"Considering you had the strength to dress yourself, I assumed you were perfectly capable of reading to yourself as well," she said stiffly.

"I am, but. . ." The teasing smile suggested. . .invoked. . . promised.

Maggie's mind whirled with the pleading gleam in his eyes. Her mutinous heart once again began its pounding. Her outrageous imagination wondered what Levi's lips would feel like against her own.

"Please. . . ," he whispered.

And Magnolia could no longer remember why she was even avoiding him. On trembling legs, she walked forward, pulled the book from his grasp, and settled into the straight-backed chair near the bed. Deftly, she opened the book as the last spears of light from the scarlet sunset filled the room. Clearing her throat, she began reading chapter one.

"Uh. . .I was on chapter four," Levi said, that spark of impishness in his eyes igniting to laughter.

Once more, Magnolia reveled in a shameless, improper thrill that this injured cowboy was blatantly flirting with her. Despite her resolve to remain stoic, she inserted her bottom lip between her teeth in an attempt to prevent a smile. Her attempts failed miserably. Hurriedly, Maggie swished the pages to chapter four and began reading,

WELL, three or four months run along, and it was well into the winter now. I had been to school most all the time and could spell and read and write just a little. . . .

But after her evening meal, after the shocking news of Uncle Cahill's letter, after enduring the heat of an exhausting day, Maggie found it necessary to stifle several unexpected yawns. Levi's magnetic charm faded as if he were wrapped in a veil of fog. The drowsiness she so wanted to earlier claim her now settled upon her with an undeniable heaviness. Gradually, her vision blurred, her speech slurred, and Magnolia decided to close her eyes for only a few seconds of respite from the long day. . . .

❧

Maggie started from her sleep when *The Adventures of Huckleberry Finn* slipped from her hand and hit the wooden floor.

"The sleeping beauty awakens," Levi whispered as her eyes adjusted to the soft glow of a flickering candle in a room darkened with the shadows of night.

"What happened? How long did I sleep?" Maggie pushed at her loose bun, attempting to regain a modicum of dignity and composure. The last thing she remembered, she had been reading to Levi and sunlight filled the room.

"I suppose Huck Finn's adventures seem pretty lame compared to ours these past days." The candle's soft glow only intensified the gleam in Levi's eyes as he playfully teased Maggie. "Ol' Twain flat-out put you to sleep."

"And you didn't have the decency to waken me?" Maggie shot back, her face warming at the thought of Levi watching her nap.

"Magnolia, you were exhausted. You needed the rest. It would have been cruel and selfish for me to disturb your slumber. Besides," he said with a grin, "if I had awakened you, I wouldn't have had the privilege of listening to you snore."

"I do *not* snore!" Maggie vehemently denied, her face heating all the more. She moved to the window and pulled back the curtain. The only other light she could see came from the saloon across the street. Surprised again at the late hour, Maggie's tone of voice switched to serious concern. "Just what time is it, anyway? Is there no news from Dr. Engle concerning Rachel?"

"The last time the mantel clock chimed, it was nine o'clock. That's nine in the evening, Magnolia, just in case you've lost all track of time. And, no, there's been no word from Dr. Engle as of yet. I don't know whether to interpret his sustained absence as a good or bad sign. What do you think, nurse?"

"It's hard to say in situations like this. We may very well not see Dr. Engle for another day. I know he won't leave Rachel until her condition is stable."

"I've been praying all day that the Lord would watch over them. It will break their hearts if this baby doesn't live. And I can't help but think that I might have brought on Rachel's suffering, with the worry and trouble I've been."

"Levi, don't," Maggie interjected, vaguely recalling her earlier attempts at indifference. "Don't say such things. You mustn't blame yourself. These kinds of problems happen to women all the time. Your situation has nothing to do with it."

Stop it, Maggie, she fiercely scolded herself. All day, Maggie had managed to keep her distance from Levi. . . until he had somehow talked her into reading to him. Now here she was showing too much interest, too much concern, too much familiarity—*again*.

"The hour is late, Levi," Maggie said firmly as she stooped to pick up the book from the floor. "And, while I am now rested, I'm certain that you need your sleep. I will retire to Dr. Engle's parlor until morning, if you don't mind. You know to ring the bell. . ."

"Wait, Magnolia," Levi caught her arm before she turned to go, and his tender touch left Magnolia trembling. "There's something I feel I must ask you while I still have the chance. You've left me in a quandary and I want to get things straight."

The sudden seriousness in Levi's voice sent Maggie's

thoughts spinning in a dozen directions, but she maintained a calm demeanor, diminutively studying her hands as he spoke.

"You've seen me at the most vulnerable time of my life and now, well, I might as well jump into this with both feet. I can't begin to tell you how many nights I prayed under the prairie stars of west Texas and asked the Lord to lead me to the woman He means for me. But never before, not until I met you, have I ever come across a woman I felt could be that special one." His gentle grip on her arm increased in fervency. Likewise, Maggie's quivering increased.

"Despite my torments and teasings, I believe that you are aware of my growing affection for you. Earlier, as you slept, I practically held my breath for fear of breaking that enchanting spell. Throughout your repose, your loveliness filled the room. I wanted to etch your beauty indelibly in my mind and I could have watched you sleep for countless hours on end."

Maggie desperately wanted to look into Levi's eyes and study the face of this man whose words had lost the cadence of a west Texas cattleman and taken on the nuance of a poet. But as Levi continued to speak, she stubbornly concentrated on her fingernails instead of basking in the warmth of his direct, admiring appraisal.

"The first moment I saw you, despite my delirium, you looked like an absolute angel to me and my appreciation of your beauty has only deepened with each passing day. But it is more than just your loveliness that attracts me to you.

"Magnolia, you and I are kindred spirits. You put your

faith to work and your compassionate heart is expressed in all you do." Levi released her arm and reached toward her face, softly stroking her cheeks. His light touch sent chills exploding throughout Maggie.

"Now, I may be totally wrong. Could be I've been alone under the stars one too many nights. Still, I feel pretty certain that you are having these same kinds of feelings for me. If I am wrong, then just look me straight in the eye and deny it.

"Look at me, Magnolia." Levi tenderly took her chin in his hand and tugged her face toward his. "Would you have me leave you alone?"

"Levi, I. . .you. . .you and I. . ." As hard as she tried, Maggie could not face his gaze. She focused on the window, just behind him instead. "We are not as alike as you seem to think. Actually, we are not anything alike. We come from two different worlds. There are things about me that, if I were to tell you, would send you runnin' the other way."

"You can't do it, can you, Magnolia?" Levi defiantly interrupted, tugging at her chin again. "You can't honestly say that you aren't drawn to me."

"In the long run, Levi, we have to look beyond. . . beyond how we feel. We must be practical. For me to even consider encouraging a relationship—with you or anyone right now—would be absurd."

"All right, Magnolia. I won't fuss with you about it anymore tonight. But don't expect me to give up on winning your heart just yet."

"Listen, Levi." Maggie stepped out of his reach. "If you insist on pinning your hopes and dreams to this relationship you want with me, I can't very well stop you. But I'm afraid you're headed for a big disappointment."

Fear gripped Maggie's heart as she swiftly turned away and scurried from the room. He definitely knew too much, even if he had no knowledge of the fresh secrets this week's cataclysmic events dropped into her life.

Crossing through the short hallway that separated Dr. Engle's professional rooms from his private quarters, Maggie noticed too late that she had neglected to carry a light with her. She passed by the dark parlor and felt her way to the kitchen, where a smoldering fire cast a red glow across the walls. After lighting a kerosene lamp, Maggie returned to the ornate parlor, careful to lock the door between the personal and professional quarters—not that she suspected Mr. Campbell would attempt any manner of ungentlemanly conduct. However, Maggie forever considered appearances. She in no way wanted a sick citizen to arrive in the night only to find the door between the quarters unlocked. More than one night she had slept on Dr. Engle's couch when he was out and a patient needed care. The township accepted this fact of Maggie's position, but Uncle Cahill had taught her to take no chances on marring her spotless reputation.

The rarely used parlor still bore the distinctive decorative touch of the deceased doctor's wife. Maggie removed her high-topped shoes and eased herself onto the red velvet sofa, thankful that the size of Widow Baker's mourning dresses did not require that Maggie wear a corset. She covered her legs with an embroidered linen lap blanket used by Mrs. Engle in the months preceding her death. A portrait of the frail, yet stately lady hung over the stone fireplace. In an attempt to shove images of Levi from her mind, Magnolia turned to one in the portrait.

Mrs. Engle had always treated Maggie with such kindness during her childhood, and the doctor's wife had been one of a precious few motherly influences upon Maggie. Without fail, Mrs. Engle delivered a large basket of pies and breads and sweets to the Alexander home each Christmas. Always tucked inside the basket was a package just for Maggie, containing some uniquely feminine thing that Uncle Cahill would never think to give. Delicate lace handkerchiefs. Real French perfume in a cut-glass bottle. A cameo broach. Tortoise-shell combs for her hair. Mrs. Engle seemed to delight in pampering Maggie, treating her like the child she never had.

As a little girl, Maggie loved visiting the Engles' home. She still cherished the memories of sitting on this very sofa, her feet dangling off the edge while she tried to behave like a little lady. Magnolia studied the portrait of the graceful, elegant Mrs. Engle, and her heart twisted for the doctor. With fresh insight, she related to the grief and despair he endured at his companion's death. How many sleepless nights since her death had Dr. Engle looked up at this portrait and longed to feel her, to speak with her once again—just as Maggie longed to speak to Uncle Cahill and feel his strong, warm hand on her shoulder.

When Mrs. Engle died, the poor doctor surely must have born an insufferable loneliness. Maggie cringed as she thought back to the comments folks all over Dogwood were making after Mrs. Engle was laid to rest. The whole citizenry seemed certain that Dr. Engle was the kind of man who simply couldn't survive without a wife. Even

Uncle Cahill had said, "It's only natural that he and the Widow Baker get hitched." Maggie knew from recent experience that, despite their good intentions, the smothering compassion of the Dogwood townsfolk often oppressed rather than uplifted.

The local matchmakers were undoubtedly in their heyday after the doctor's mourning period, when he actually began to call on the middle-aged widow, Sarah Baker. Bess Tucker, the buxom, red-cheeked clerk at the general store, had immediately stocked a bolt of exquisitely patterned silk in anticipation of a wedding dress for Widow Baker.

But the good people of Dogwood were sorely disappointed when Doc Engle's courting of the Widow Baker came to an abrupt end. Within hours of the apparent breakup, speculations began to fly all over town as to what had caused the lovers' feud. The tension between Luke Engle and Sarah Baker could hardly go unnoticed. They deliberately avoided one another, despite the inconvenience of doing so. No matter how hard their friends and neighbors pried, neither would reveal the root of their dispute. Both the doctor and the widow refused to even discuss the other party. Quite obviously, they didn't want their private lives to continue as a topic of public debate. Even Maggie, who found herself in close association with both Dr. Engle and Widow Baker, was unable to broach the subject for fear of offending them.

"I wonder if Dr. Engle even shared with *you* the reason for their feud?"

As Maggie addressed the portrait of Mrs. Engle, the

finely etched lips seemed to curl upwards into a hint of a grin.

And I wonder what drastic measures I'll have to take in order to squelch the rumor now circulating about me. Undoubtedly, eyebrows all over town were already raised in question concerning the prospects of a deepening relationship between Levi and Maggie. Whenever Maggie walked through town, she sensed that her life was the most popular discussion around.

The dear folks of Dogwood apparently saw the time of mourning as the perfect opportunity to find romance. In all likelihood, nosy Bess at the general store had already charged an order for a bolt of silk brocade to Maggie's account.

Magnolia grimaced at the thought before breaking into a smile. She, too, would put into practice the tactics of Dr. Engle and Widow Baker. She could turn a deaf ear to the town gossips' comments just as skillfully as they. Her Dogwood audience was just one more reason to sidestep any sort of a relationship with Levi. If they ever learned about Uncle Cahill's past, the township would certainly associate any breakup in a relationship with Levi as a logical consequence of Mr. Campbell's disdain for a woman of Magnolia's upbringing. But if there were no relationship to end, that would give the citizens of Dogwood one less avenue of gossip.

With fresh resolve, Maggie pledged to scorn all Mr. Campbell's advances. She picked up her book and stared at the pages of *Huckleberry Finn* until the words blurred together like a newspaper in the rain. Despite the fact that she had napped for several hours under Levi's watchful care, the exhaustion of the week once more evoked a pall of drowsiness upon her mind. Magnolia slept soundly throughout the night's remainder.

❧

The next morning, Maggie rubbed her cheeks in an effort to rouse herself from her deep sleep. Natural light overpowered the pale glow of the kerosene flame as she folded the lap blanket and began the task of washing her face, combing her hair, and freshening up. She was certain that she had heard the floorboards in the entryway creak under the weight of Dr. Engle's heavy boots as he walked toward the kitchen.

Certain that the well-meaning doctor was planning to make some of his infamously awful coffee, Maggie hurried into the kitchen, determined to take over before everyone was forced to drink the acrid liquid.

"Good morning. Glad to see you made it home." Maggie laid her hand on the doctor's stooped shoulders as he gripped the sides of the drysink and stared blindly out the window.

"Hello, Maggie. I didn't expect to see you here. How's our patient?" he asked listlessly.

Magnolia stiffened against the pleasure the very sound of Levi's name evoked. "I haven't checked on him this morning, but he appeared much stronger when I saw him late last night. From the looks of things, he's doing better than you are." A certain dread rushed upon Maggie. She had seen the doctor this grim many times. . .many times when he had lost a patient. Magnolia swallowed against the lump in her throat. "Rachel. . .is she. . ."

Dr. Engle appraised his nurse through tear-reddened

eyes. "You know, Maggie, I brought Rachel into this world and it pains me somethin' fierce to see her suffering so. She lost the baby. And both she and Travis are taking it pretty hard."

eight

Furrowed lines of worry shadowed the doctor's face, making him appear older than his sixty years. "Maggie, would you mind running out to their farm later today and checking up on Rachel? I think she could really use another woman to talk to right about now."

"Certainly, Dr. Engle." Magnolia's heart wrenched with the agony Rachel must be facing. Perhaps Maggie's own recent loss would bond them together as only grief can bond. "You know I'll do whatever I can to help Rachel. It's all just so sad." She flipped the latch on the window above the drysink and pushed against the two wood-framed panes. With a faint squeak, they swung outward to allow fresh air into the already stuffy room. The gentle morning breeze that cooled Maggie's cheeks brought a welcome relief to the kitchen's fire-warmed air. Nonetheless, the bright sun promised to produce yet another hot Texas day with a heavy blanket of humidity. Her black moiré dress absorbed heat like a cast-iron stove, and Magnolia could feel her hair already curling against her temples.

"There's more to it than I had the courage to admit to Rachel and Travis today." The doctor absently toyed with the watch chain hanging from his vest pocket. "I couldn't bear to bring any more bad news, but I suspect that Rachel will never be able to carry a child to full term. She seems terribly small."

Maggie turned to Dr. Engle, shaking her head. "Life just doesn't seem fair sometimes does it? When folks like Rachel and Travis long for a child and would make wonderful parents, yet are deprived of that privilege, and then young girls like Louella Simpson, who has no husband and no hope of providing a stable home, are strapped with the heavy burden of an impending child."

Dr. Engle raised an eyebrow in question. "I'm afraid I'm not familiar with a Louella Simpson."

"Oh, I'm sorry. I guess the two of you haven't met." Maggie busied herself in stoking the fire, then filled the coffeepot with well water from the wooden bucket beside the drysink. "Louella will be in to see you very shortly. She's a kind, gentle spirit with a good many problems. Louella's going to need some assistance in delivering a child very soon. I'll let her explain her situation. I don't want to betray any confidences. But I do think you'll find her delightful despite her compromised position."

"Ah, yes, she must be the messenger Levi spoke of yesterday morning," Dr. Engle recalled as he reached for the coffee tin. "But since we're talking of young women needing help, how are you doing, Maggie?"

Gently, Maggie removed the aging blue coffee tin from the doctor's weary hands. "As good as can be expected, I suppose, Dr. Engle. Really, that's one of the reasons I've kept myself busy around here. I can't let myself stop and think about all that's gone on this week. I'm afraid I'd go crazy."

"I know it's not much comfort now," Dr. Engle said, "but the pain does subside. Take it from me. I know. I have to tell you, though, I'll never get over missing my wife." He rubbed his jaw, covered by a day's gray stubble, and settled at the kitchen table. The doctor propped his elbow on the table and rested his forehead against his hand.

Dreading the resulting heat, Maggie inserted a couple of small sticks onto the glowing coals, then scooped two heaping spoonfuls of coffee into the pot and set it on the metal rack over the crackling fire.

"I'm so tired, I almost forgot," Dr. Engle said. "Travis insisted on sending me home with a basket full of fresh eggs and a slab of bacon from the pig he butchered last week. Do you think you could fry some up and feed our patient a hearty breakfast today? Your fine cookin' might do me good as well."

"Just leave the breakfast to me, Dr. Engle." Maggie crossed the room and uncovered a large wicker basket sitting by the back door. "You rest a spell. You've been working much too hard."

"I'm beginning to think that I'm getting too old for this business. I had always planned to retire when I started delivering a second generation of babies, and Rachel's baby would have been the first in that category. Now, it looks like I'll have to wait a little longer to take down my shingle."

Dr. Engle's shoulders heaved with the weight of a heavy sigh as he continued. "It seems like our work comes in spurts, doesn't it, Maggie? Remember just a couple of weeks ago, we were sitting in my office playing checkers for lack of anything better to do? Now we're hoppin' to stay on top of things.

"I suppose we'd better organize our day. After breakfast,

before you head out to see Rachel, I'd like to see the constable and find out if he was able to track down those bandits. I'm committed to finding those scoundrels who murdered your uncle. If Constable Parker can't find 'em, I'm tempted to go on a manhunt—or a womanhunt—myself.

"You have heard, haven't you?" The doctor's eyes widened with question. "Yesterday, Levi spotted one of those women bandits leaving the saloon with some scroungy man."

"Yes, Widow Baker gave me the word. But I'm curious to hear if the constable's search has met with success. Does he still believe that the train holdup and Uncle Cahill's murder were the work of the same team?"

"The constable thinks maybe they left the train robbery and fell upon your uncle's house, bent on taking more money. That old homestead isn't very far from the place where the train stopped after the robbery, you know."

Flashes of panic, fear, and uncertainty skirted through Maggie's mind. She had been so consumed with her uncle's lifelong deception that she had given little thought to the fact that his murderer—or murderers—were still at large, despite the constable's warnings. She wasn't quite sure which would be worse, allowing a killer to go free or sitting in a murder trial, telling all regarding the questionable circumstances surrounding her uncle's death. Could the crooked ex-lawman, mentioned in her uncle's letter, have joined forces with the women bandits who robbed the train? No other suspicious stranger had been seen in town. She shuddered to imagine the spectacle of their trial. The whispered gossip around Dogwood concerning her and Levi would drastically dim in comparison to the buzz created by the revelations about her "upright" uncle.

"Have I upset you with all this talk, Maggie? You're looking pale," Dr. Engle asked as he grabbed a potholder and carefully removed the coffeepot from the rack over the fire.

"No. . .no, I'm fine. Just fine. I'm just thinking about those outlaws running free and all. Can I get you some sugar for your coffee?"

"No thanks. I think I'll have it black, if you can call this coffee," he grumbled, filling a stoneware mug to the brim. "It's more like water if you ask me."

Out of politeness to her employer and her elder, Maggie remained silent. However, a noise in the hallway dashed away all vestiges of the former conversation. Both Maggie and Dr. Engle turned toward the sound to see Levi pushing against the kitchen's swinging doors.

"You know, I'm pretty handy around a kitchen. And folks say that my coffee tastes mighty good."

Maggie gaped at the sight of him, decked out like a cowboy in the new jeans and denim shirt, with a sun-faded red bandanna around his neck. His arm still rested in the sling, and he looked every bit the wounded hero. Furthermore, his tanned skin spoke of good health rather than the sickly complexion of an invalid. At that moment, Maggie thought she had never seen a more handsome man. The embers in Levi's emerald eyes blazed when he playfully winked at Magnolia. The good doctor produced a humorous grunt, and Maggie quickly concentrated on the eggs she planned to scramble. Despite her pledges to remain distant with Levi, a delightful tremble passed through her midsection.

Levi passed her to approach the doctor, and Maggie's fingers trembled as she cracked several eggs into a wooden mixing bowl. "You're right. That *does* look like water." Magnolia glanced toward the pair to witness Levi scrutinizing the doctor's steaming coffee mug. With his left hand, he took the coffeepot from the exhausted doctor. "Do you mind if I make a fresh pot? I like my coffee strong enough to hold a spoon upright."

"I knew we must have something in common, boy," the doctor said with a tired smirk. "If Maggie had her way, I'd be sippin' watery coffee 'til my dyin' day."

"I'll take a cup of that before you throw it out." Magnolia hurriedly wiped her hands on a dishtowel before relieving Levi of the pot.

The men chuckled.

"Looks to me like you need to be moving along to your brother's ranch now, Levi," the doctor said as Maggie filled a mug with the fragrant coffee.

She felt Levi's observation as he reluctantly agreed with the doctor. Instinctively, Magnolia glanced toward him to see desperation and longing flitting across his features. If Levi left, when would the two of them ever see each other again? He might very easily complete his visit and return to west Texas without so much as another word with Maggie. *So let it be*, she thought. *The less I'm with him, the less likely I'll be to get hurt.* Regardless of the flutter he created in her midsection with his audacious winks, regardless of her growing attachment to him, the sad reality remained: Magnolia was afraid to trust, and he would be afraid to love once he learned her background.

"Well, I can see my assistance in the kitchen is no longer

required," Dr. Engle said a bit too sagely. "I believe I'll try to catch a few minutes of shut-eye if you two will excuse me for a while."

"No, Dr. Engle," Maggie rushed frantically. "You can't leave until you've had your breakfast. Sit down here and wait for just a minute while I scramble these eggs and fry up the bacon." Reaching for the cast-iron skillet hanging on a hook beside the fireplace, she intensely hoped her employer would take the hint. Maggie could have hugged him when he returned to his chair and said, "I guess my ol' stomach is grumbling a bit."

While Maggie turned her attention to the eggs and bacon, Levi settled across from Dr. Engle. "I'm afraid to ask, Doc," Levi said seriously. "But, how is Rachel doing?"

"Levi, I. . ." The doctor hesitated, and his voice grew thick with emotion. "I've got sad news to report."

"Is Rachel—"

"No, no. Rachel's fine. But the baby. . .the baby didn't make it. She just came too early."

The three of them remained silent as the fog of death seemed to settle upon the room, forever banishing any attempt at cheerfulness. Magnolia completed the breakfast, and the kitchen filled with the mouth-watering aroma of fresh bacon. At last, she heaped plates with the scrambled eggs and bacon, but even the scrumptious feast couldn't abate the despondent mood that had settled upon them. Levi stared in stunned silence at the candle, sitting in the middle of the table. Dr. Engle rubbed his eyes. And Rachel blinked rapidly against tears, feeling as if she had lost Uncle Cahill all over again.

As she prepared to serve the breakfast, Maggie bumped

the coffeepot, left sitting on the kitchen counter. With resignation, she grabbed the gray-specked pot and turned toward the back door, intent on discarding the mellow brew. On second thought, she just reached for the blue coffee tin and dumped an obnoxious amount of grounds into the existing liquid. She grabbed the dipper from the well bucket and measured more water into the coffeepot. For the kind of concoction the doctor and Levi liked, it would make little difference if part of it were warmed-up leftovers. With the sound of metal against metal, Magnolia deposited the coffeepot on the cooking rack and picked up the breakfast plates.

"Well, I haven't had much of a chance to get to know Rachel," Levi said somberly. "But I think, by all Travis says, that I'll like her. She's been through a pretty rough year—not unlike you, Magnolia, both of you losing a parent and all." Levi and the doctor nodded their thanks as Maggie set the plates in front of them.

But before she could turn away, Levi's sympathetic appraisal bore into her very soul. The rivulets of perspiration down her back seemed more a result of the warmth in Levi's eyes than her work at the fireplace. Magnolia held her breath as their gaze lengthened. She wondered what life would be like, sharing breakfast with this man every morning. She pondered the possibility that one day they might marry and, like Travis and Rachel, would discover their love had blossomed into another life. Terrified that Levi would perceive the shameful direction of her thoughts, Maggie abruptly walked back to the fireplace to remove the bubbling coffee.

As Dr. Engle blessed their food, she closed her eyes and

delayed the task of pouring the inky liquid into two thick mugs until his "amen" freed her to proceed.

"Doctor, I must confess," Levi said, "that my brother's loss now leaves me in a quandary about what I should do." He cut a heel of bread from the ever-present loaf on the table, then filled his mouth with a forkful of eggs.

"I understand," the doctor replied as Magnolia set a cup of the detestable brew in front of each man.

"Like you said, it's time for me to move along, but I don't want to intrude on Travis and Rachel at this delicate time. Can you direct me to a good hotel in town?"

Dr. Engle looked at Maggie with questioning eyes. "Does Widow Baker have any extra room to spare at her place right now?"

As she floundered for a reply, Magnolia's earlier, frantic musings about never seeing Levi again now haunted her. What was worse? Never seeing him again or having him in the same boardinghouse. . .always in contact with him but forever keeping her distance. For a fleeting moment she considered the possibility that the two men had previously plotted this subversive scheme. Had Levi confided to Dr. Engle his intentions to win Maggie's heart? Immediately, she dismissed the notion. Dr. Engle, forever the tease, would have undoubtedly leaked any such information to the young lady whom he treated like a daughter.

She steeled herself against the temptation to lie about the widow's vacancies. That would do nothing but hinder the kind lady's livelihood and grieve the Lord. "Yes, Doc Engle. I think Mrs. Baker does have an opening," Magnolia said with resignation. "That fella Slim Rogers left to go back east last week. His room is still available as far as I know." Shoulders drooping, Maggie stepped back toward the kitchen counter with intent to place her own plate on the table and eat. But her churning stomach rejected the very sight of the food she had labored to prepare.

Gripping the kitchen counter, Magnolia debated what to do. She pressed her lips into a decisive line and determined to fill the drysink with the breakfast dishes. Magnolia would douse them with the water now boiling in the iron pot that hung over the cooking rack and leave the mess until later. While the men enjoyed their meal, she busied herself with the myriad of other chores a kitchen demands and sipped her coffee.

Finally, the men finished, and she began the task of clearing the table. "As soon as I finish here, Levi, I'll get my things and accompany you to Widow Baker's," she mumbled, frantically attempting to hide her desperation.

"Maggie, would you also inquire of Constable Parker any news of the bandits?" Dr. Engle said. "I certainly would like an update, as I'm sure you and Levi would." He glanced from her to Levi and back, as if he were contemplating much more than the status of the outlaw chase.

"Of course," Maggie said mechanically.

"Well, if the two of you will excuse me. . . ," the doctor said discreetly. Maggie could only imagine what he must be thinking. "I'll retire for a spell." His chair scraped against the floor.

Squelching the desire to run after the wise doctor, Maggie hopelessly watched him push his way through the swinging doors and vanish into the hallway. Like a woman on a grievous mission, she gathered the remaining dirty dishes from the table and piled them in the drysink, just as planned. But she hadn't planned on how to deal with Levi's nonplussed appraisal. Her legs trembling, Magnolia grabbed a thick towel, stepped to the fire, and struggled to retrieve the kettle of boiling water from its hook. Although manning the iron pot was usually the doctor's chore, Maggie's own weakness left her exasperated. The more she struggled to maneuver the kettle, the more frustrated she became. The last thing she wanted was the close proximity of Levi's assistance. But the sound of his chair scooting away from the table preceded his presence by only seconds. With his free left hand, he effortlessly took the kettle from Maggie and poured its contents over the dirty dishes in the sink.

Refusing to look at him, she said, "If you'll gather your things, I'll meet you at the front door."

"Would you prefer I find another place to stay?" he asked quietly. "I certainly don't want to burden you."

His words demanded Maggie's full attention. She looked upward to find him only inches from her, and his unexpected grin left her speechless.

"Y–You are–aren't a–a burden," she stammered as her mind spun with his nearness. For the first time in Maggie's determination to keep Mr. Levi Campbell at arm's length, she wondered if she could actually succeed. Would her tattered, lonely heart override her common sense? Would she find herself swept away by this charming man's obvious attempts to woo her, despite her better judgment?

"Well, in that case. . ." He paused to meaningfully clear his throat, his smile taking on the nuance of victory. "Would you mind if I tagged along when you go to my brother's? I'd like to visit with Travis while you're tending to Rachel's physical needs."

"Of course. That's understandable. But I'm afraid that you may overdo. You're not that strong yet. You still need plenty of rest." Maggie attempted to sound coldly professional in hopes of masking the quiver in her voice. But the thought of sitting next to him in a buggy left her feeling anything but coldly professional.

"I'll be fine," he said, that flirtatious grin ever in place. "What man wouldn't be with a lady like you at his side?"

"Levi—" She gripped the counter once again and watched the steam rising off the breakfast dishes. "*Don't*," she said firmly. "I already told you. . .I–I. . .there are things you don't know—things better left unsaid. Please honor my request to keep our interactings professional." Doing her best to present him with a stony stare, she silently demanded he discontinue his pursuit of her.

A gray disappointment washed across Levi's features, snuffing out the glow of expectation, molding his grin into a disheartened wilt. "Of course," he said as if she had slapped him. "I'll abide by your wishes, Miss Alexander."

"Thank you, Mr. Campbell," she replied stiffly, although her heart ached with the pain so evident in his eyes. "I'll retrieve my things and head over to the livery for Doc's horses and buggy. All I have is an opened wagon, and we'll need his covered buggy for protection against the sun. I'll meet you out front in, say, ten minutes. Does that sound agreeable to you?"

"I'll be there," Levi said solemnly.

nine

Within thirty minutes, Levi had settled his belongings at the boardinghouse, much to the pleasure of Mrs. Baker, whom he fully delighted. Magnolia and Levi then rode in silence to the constable's office, where she tethered the horses to the hitching post. As Maggie surreptitiously observed Levi climbing from the carriage, her heart beat with regret. Regret that her circumstances prevented the slightest chance of a relationship with the poetic cowboy. Even now, as he stepped onto the boardwalk, Magnolia knew she would never forget him. Never. Even if she lived to be ninety and the whole frontier separated them. Levi Campbell would be indelibly etched upon her memory. He hadn't so much as looked her way since those tense moments in the kitchen. And even as he pushed open the lawman's door, Levi maintained an impassive face and emotional distance. But wasn't that what she wanted?

The temperature inside the windowless building was significantly cooler due to its thick concrete walls. With the smells of mildew encompassing her, Maggie felt as if the cool air penetrated straight to her heart. Levi was indeed giving her what she had insisted upon for their relationship, but Maggie ached with his conformity to her demands. Part of her much preferred the dapper winks and adoring smile to this indifference. Nevertheless, her common sense demanded that the more formal their relationship, the safer.

Levi cleared his throat in an attempt to awaken the dozing constable, who leaned back in his chair with his feet propped on the desk. Uncle Cahill's old coonhound, Ruff, jumped up from a worn rag rug beside the constable's desk and woofed an excited greeting to Maggie, his familiar friend. The hound's tail flipped furiously as he barked. Startled from the catnap, Parker jumped. Rubbing his eyes, he slowly stood and produced a sheepish smile.

"It's been a long night," he said through a yawn.

"Do you have word on the bandits?" Levi asked.

"Word? Son, ain't you heard? We nabbed 'em last night!" The constable broke into a grin. "That's what they get for dependin' on the bottle too hard. Best I can figure, they came into town durin' the night because they had to have some whiskey. And that stuff made 'em lose all good judgment." The wall lantern's flickering shadows only increased the intensity of the lines, etching his weathered face.

A sense of both expectation and dread engulfed Magnolia. Were these the bandits who killed her uncle?

"Thanks to the keen nose of ol' Ruff here. . ." The constable stooped to give the panting dog a scratch behind his ears. "I not only caught me the two women who we suspect held up the train, but I nabbed a third suspicious character as well. I figure he's the man you saw leaving the saloon with the redhead, Levi. He was holed up with those gals in a cave along White Woman Creek. Believe it or not, he used to be a deputy in Dallas, and I've got a "Wanted" poster for his return. Seems he used his influence as a lawman to help himself to some of the bank's money. I wouldn't be surprised if he was the mastermind behind all their evil schemes."

Maggie reeled with the implications. Her mind racing, she stared at the hodgepodge of "Wanted" posters lining one of the whitewashed walls. Uncle Cahill's murderer was an ex-lawman. This could very well be the beginnings of the process that she dreaded. The trial of her uncle's attacker. The revelation of Cahill Alexander's true identity. The loss of her good standing among the community. Her empty stomach twisted in nausea.

With the toe of his boot, the constable slid a tray full of dirty dishes from his path and approached Maggie and Levi. "I tell you what, those three put up quite a fight. I waited 'til they were sleepin' and took their guns away. But even unarmed, it was like corallin' bobcats to capture 'em." All traces of exhaustion left the lawman as he recounted the thrill of his most recent chase.

"I believe that," Levi said dryly. "Those two women are about the toughest two females I've ever met in my life."

"You feel up to identifying them?" The wiry constable paused to scrutinize Levi. "I didn't think for one minute to ask how you're doin'. Has that doctor turned you out now?"

"Yes. And I'm well on the mend. Enough that I'd like to take a look at those bandits. The sooner I make sure you've nabbed the right ones, the easier I can rest."

Grunting his approval, Constable Parker grabbed a brass key ring from its peg on the side of his desk. Motioning for Levi and Maggie to follow, he walked to the locked ironware door separating the jail cells from the outer office.

"Maggie, you can come along, too. I'd like you to see if you recognize any of 'em. I have a hunch you might of seen 'em around your place before."

Reluctantly, she joined Levi behind the constable as he inserted the key and turned the lock with an abundance of squeaks and clatters. "You know, it's a good thing the folks of Dogwood had enough sense to build two jail cells instead of one. This isn't the first time I've had 'em both filled," the lawman announced as he shoved open the creaking door and led the way into the dimly lighted quarters.

Immediately, Maggie's nostrils flared with the invasion of a repugnant stench. She looked to Levi, whose repulsed expression matched her own reaction. Two creatures bearing only a slight resemblance to females sat on the cots in the first cell. Neither bothered to look up as the trio entered the corridor in front of their cubicle.

Someone had hung a curtain to provide a modicum of privacy between their cell and the next one, where a solitary man lay on his cot, staring at the ceiling. Intent on examining the prisoners, Maggie crunched across something that felt like gravel and glue under her high-topped shoes. She glanced down to see shards of a shattered pottery bowl mixed with lumps of drying, gray oatmeal.

As distasteful a sight as the oatmeal presented, Magnolia turned her attention to the man. Her knees trembling, she attempted to find one thing familiar about him. But the lean angles of his granitelike face were those of a stranger. The only evidence against him would be her uncle's claim that his murderer was once a lawman.

A new rush of nausea assaulted Maggie. Nausea, accompanied by panic. She would be forced to read Uncle

Cahill's letter in court. There would be no other way to convict the man who murdered him. And in convicting the murderer, Maggie would also be stating her own sentence. A sentence of shame. A sentence of scandal. A sentence of solitude.

"Whatcha botherin' us for?" one of the female creatures snarled. Her flame red hair, an unkempt mass of tangles, cascaded down her back as she glared at them. She tilted her head and spit a stream of tobacco on the floor near the iron bars. Her mud-crusted shirt and jeans looked as if she had been wearing them a year. "You'd think they ain't never seen the likes of a lady before," she mocked.

Her grimy cell mate produced a sarcastic snort and shoved a handful of dark, oily hair from her face.

"I wanted to give these folks a chance to see if y'all are the ones who've done 'em such harm," Constable Parker barked, looking toward Levi for confirmation.

Levi produced an affirmative nod.

"The gentleman here, you may recall, is the guy you shot and threw from the train. And his lady companion, why, her only livin' relative was murdered, and I suspect one or all of ya were in on it."

"We ain't no murderers," groused the redhead. Her companion cast a snake-eyed stare at Maggie as her partner in crime continued. "I told you before, we don't know nothin' about no murders. We was only tryin' to hold up the train. We needed some cash to make our way out to California. We didn't even aim to really hurt this feller. He just got in our way."

"Well, you admit to that, at least," the constable threw back. "That alone should make the circuit judge's trip worth his while. But your companion there ain't uttered a word yet, and you'll have to do some pretty fast talkin' to convince the judge the three of ya weren't the ones to kill Cahill Alexander."

"I'll tell you again and again, we didn't kill nobody," the redhead growled.

"Yeah, yeah. That's just what I'd expect you to say. I'd probably say the same if I were lookin' at swingin' from a hangman's noose."

Magnolia felt the scrutiny of their masculine partner, and she cringed as she met his gaze through the wall lantern's flickering shadows. He evaluated her in a most forward and lewd manner. . .in a manner that suggested he had seen her before. . .in a manner that made her thankful the good Lord had prevented her from being at the farm the day of her uncle's murder. Certainly, this dastardly creature must have been the ex-lawman her uncle mentioned. There could be no other explanation.

"Circuit Judge Hamilton should be through here in a couple of weeks, Levi," Parker said. "The trial shouldn't take long. I'm assumin' you're planning on being in these parts till then?"

"Yes."

The evil man's lecherous perusal added to the evilness radiating from the lawless trio and thoroughly repulsed Maggie. She rushed back into the outer office. The revolting odor following her, Magnolia hurried past the constable's desk to the front door. Flinging it open, she inhaled great gulps of the warm morning air. The resignation that she would soon be forced to share Uncle Cahill's humiliating secrets only added to her distress.

Who was this ex-lawman turned bad? Uncle Cahill said he no longer went by the name Dallas Blankenship. Was that the name on his "Wanted" poster? She debated how best to inquire of the constable concerning these matters without giving away her uncle's disgraceful history.

"Are you all right?" Levi asked from close behind. The light hand on her left shoulder spoke of the concern in his voice, a concern that broke through all of Magnolia's tumultuous musings. Levi. Levi Campbell. He was a kind man. A considerate man. A man who would willingly take her heart, were she to extend it. Should she confide in him? Should she burden his broad shoulders with her growing problems? Would he indeed reject her as she had previously assumed?

The morning's humidity combined with the tornado of varying, tumultuous thoughts caused her pulse to pound in her temples, and she passionately hoped this wasn't the beginning of one of her blinding headaches. *Oh, Lord, guide me. Please show me the right thing to do,* Maggie pleaded as she turned to face Levi.

"Fine. I'm fine," she answered. "The whole thing just got to be too much for me."

"If that rascal wasn't behind bars, I'd have thrashed him," Levi said through clenched teeth.

Maggie's cheeks flared with heat at the thought that Levi understood what the horrid man had been thinking. Not daring to raise her gaze above his shirt's top button, she muttered a polite, although embarrassed "thank you."

Constable Parker arrived at their side. "I'm sorry if that was too much for ya, Miss Maggie," he said, a father's concern in his eyes. "But I had to know if you might recognize that man."

"To my knowledge, I've never seen him before," Maggie replied, groping for any natural way to inquire about seeing the man's "Wanted" poster. "But. . .I was wonderin'. . . ," she hedged.

The constable raised his bushy, graying brows.

"Would it be possible for me to see his 'Wanted' poster. It might. . .might give me a better. . .better idea of his features. The cell was rather shadowed, and. . ." At least that was true. Perhaps she might recognize him once she saw a clear drawing. Groping for any possibilities, she held her breath as Parker produced the "Wanted" poster from the mound of clutter on his desk.

"Here 'tis," he said, handing the paper to Maggie.

Anxiously, she pored over the unfamiliar image, then traced her finger along the list of six aliases. The name "Dallas Blankenship" was not mentioned. However, the fact that he had used six other assumed names left her concluding that he must have dreamed up a few pseudonyms that were left off the poster.

Feeling the men watching her, Magnolia licked her lips and shook her head. "I can't say that I've ever seen him before, Constable." Cautiously, she glanced at the lawman, who suspiciously eyed her. Maggie, fatigued from the whole ordeal, turned back to the ajar door. Lifting her moiré skirt, she stepped onto the boardwalk and headed toward the doctor's black carriage.

The men's congenial adieus did little to disrupt Maggie's heavy deliberation. Never had she been so trapped between decisions, decisions that would alter her life and the life of another. Pausing by the doctor's hooded buggy, she contemplated her options. If she read Uncle Cahill's letter in court, that man in the jail cell would undoubtedly hang, and Maggie's reputation would hang with him. If she didn't read the letter. . . . She squelched the very notion and made her final decision. Magnolia would do what was right, what was lawful. She would read the letter. She would also begin considering the possibilities of leaving Dogwood, for after the trial, she would assuredly be stripped of her glowing reputation.

She began embarking the carriage, only to have Levi gently grip her upper arm. Too emotionally spent to stop him, Magnolia allowed his assistance and settled on the padded bench. When he untethered the horses, Magnolia scolded herself for forgetting that simple task.

"Are you sure you're all right, Magnolia?" he asked. Walking back to her side, he placed the reins in her hands.

Her pulse quickened with the natural way Levi had fallen back into addressing her by her given name. "Yes. I'm fine. I'll be fine."

Levi walked around the buggy, pulled himself up with his good arm, and settled beside her. "We don't have to visit Travis's place just yet. I'm certain the doctor would understand if you—"

"No," Maggie said firmly. "My professional obligations lie with Rachel now. I mustn't let Dr. Engle down."

"If only you were as concerned about letting me down," he said, his barely discernible voice taking on the subtleties of poetry.

His words of adoration tugged Magnolia ever closer to the point of casting aside all her perfectly sensible reasons for not capitulating to Levi's romantic intentions. But her momentary vacillation was soon swept aside by her fears.

Her fears of trusting. Her fears of his abandonment.

"Mr. Campbell," she snapped, turning to face him. But instead of words of rebuttal, only silence settled between them. Silence, and the enchantment of a man thoroughly smitten. Maggie gulped as Levi's focus hungrily settled upon her lips.

"Magnolia?" he whispered.

Under his hypnotic gaze, Maggie forgot they were sitting on Dogwood's Main Street. And her earlier, immodest musings about what his lips might feel like against hers rushed back, more potent than before. As if an invisible current tugged her toward him, Maggie leaned forward, only a breath of an inch. Levi's eyes widened with surprise as he gently reached to stroke her cheek. An explosion of tingles cascaded down her cheek. A new depth of awareness. A sudden realization that shaking Levi Campbell might be much harder than she had ever imagined.

The sound of slowing footsteps jolted Magnolia back to reality—back to the fact that they were, indeed, sitting in clear view of public eyes. When she glanced toward the boardwalk to see to whom the footsteps belonged, the vexed Magnolia wanted to faint with mortification. For the buxom, ruddy-cheeked Bess Tucker gawked as if she had caught Levi actually kissing Maggie.

Compressing her lips, Magnolia tugged the reins to the left, and the horses responded with a jolt. Curtly, she nodded toward Bess and could only imagine what the quilting rings would be saying by the week's end. Skillfully, Maggie guided the carriage past Dogwood's familiar landmarks and into the tunnel of trees that covered the lane leading to the Campbell farm. As a child, Maggie had ridden down this road countless times, nestled by her uncle Cahill's side. Despite the tension still vibrating between her and Levi, a sense of deep comfort settled over Maggie. A sense of knowing that Uncle Cahill would have liked Levi Campbell.

But what does that matter? a pragmatic voice demanded. *Uncle Cahill was a former outlaw who lied to you. You couldn't trust him, and you can't trust Levi!*

But a softer voice suggested, *You have not once prayed about the Lord's will in your acquaintance with Levi. Why not relinquish your fears to God?*

Thus, the conflicting thoughts raged war within Magnolia. As they approached the farm of her childhood, she longed more than ever to feel Levi's strong arms around her, to share her anxieties with this wounded hero who had attempted to stand between two bandits and the train passengers. Would a man of such valor be the sort to abandon a woman for whom he cared because of her family's scandalous background?

No, but neither did Uncle Cahill seem an ex-criminal! You mustn't trust again!

Overcome with the internal turmoil, Magnolia realized she would be of no use whatsoever to Rachel in her current state of internal upheaval. She needed to calm her raging emotions and resume her professional demeanor before approaching the distraught mother whose infant had died. She knew only one Source that could calm her nerves.

"We're. . .we're coming to Uncle Cahill's farm. W–would you mind if we paused there for just a moment?" she stammered. Simply addressing Levi seemed to bring back that moment when he had stroked her cheek. "Travis and Rachel's ranch is just around the bend, and. . .and I would like to seek a moment. . .moment of prayer before approachin' Rachel. I. . .I need nothing short of divine wisdom. I can't imagine what she must feel like."

"Certainly," Levi replied as naturally as if he had never thought of kissing her. "I'd enjoy seeing where you grew up."

At last they reached the scenic lane leading to the Alexander farm, and Maggie guided the horses onto the circular drive. She brought the buggy to a halt between the yard full of pines and the porch on which she had often sat while listening to the pond frogs and whippoorwills' melodious chorus. Before she could gather her skirts to disembark, Levi clamored from the buggy, rounded the back, and appeared at her side, his left hand extended, his gaze as ardent as it had been in town.

Magnolia wavered between accepting his proffered help and unceremoniously scrambling out on the opposite side. But Levi stepped nearer and gently wrapped her hand in the warmth of his. Her grip on the reins relaxed. The flames in her soul glowed ever the brighter. And she regarded only one man. . .one longing. . .one possibility. The man: Levi Campbell. The longing: Maggie desired his kiss, desired the assurance of his strong arms, despite all better judgment. The possibility: Levi possessed every intent of continuing that magic moment that started in town.

As she descended the buggy with his assistance, each second turned to a moment of mystery. A moment of expectation. A moment of enchantment. She stepped to the ground and stood only inches from him. Magnolia peered upward to once more see his gaze trail to her lips.

"Magnolia. . .," he whispered. "I—"

With the mocking birds frolicking in the pines, she leaned forward but a fraction, yet enough to grant Levi full permission to wrap his arm around her and tug her closer. Maggie felt as if the world itself stopped spinning in that mystical moment. And she sensed. . .she sensed she was coming home. Home, to Levi's open arms.

Gingerly, he tightened his left arm around her, pulling Maggie as close as the sling would allow. "Ah, Magnolia," he whispered against her ear. "How often have I dreamed of this very moment. . .of holding you. . .of the softness of your hair against my cheek. . .," he uttered as if he were reading the most elegant of poems. "And. . .and I know you—for whatever reason—you have become unsure of me."

Magnolia swallowed hard, her eyes filling with the warm waters of misgivings. "I'm just so scared," she rasped.

"Yes, I know. I see it every time I look at you, but if you could just bring yourself to tell me why, I—"

Abruptly, she tore herself from his embrace. And with a broken sob, Maggie ran. She ran from the dread of telling Levi the truth. She ran from the horror that he might reject her once he knew of her uncle's dishonorable past. She ran from the Gentle Voice that again insisted she should pray and trust. . .trust and pray. Yet her distant point of destination ironically became the apple orchard, the one place of solitude where she had met the Lord on many glorious occasions. Perhaps that Gentle Voice was right. Perhaps Maggie's answer to all of her turmoil lay in the embrace of Jesus.

However, the presence of a lone horseman, cantering up

the lane, distracted Maggie from her goal and she immediately stopped. Biting her bottom lip, she forced the tears into abeyance and scrubbed against her cheeks, attempting to gain control of her raw emotions before addressing Jed Sweeney.

ten

"I was hoping I'd find you here, Miss Alexander." Jed Sweeney reined his ebony steed to a restless stop within feet of Magnolia. His shoulder-length black hair hung in feathery wisps under a black derby that rested lightly over his brow. Sweeney was a tall, lean man with broad shoulders. In his white, starched shirt and black riding britches, he could have easily been taken for a banker or lawyer, save the length of his hair and the measured way he bit into the ever-present pencil-thin cigar.

With her hand, she shaded her eyes against the mid-morning sun and noticed Sweeney's keen eyes taking in the carriage and Levi. He most certainly had seen Maggie running, and she couldn't help but wonder what he must think. Swiftly, her mind trailed to Louella. . .to her plight. . .to the cold-hearted manner with which Jed Sweeney had dismissed her.

"What can I help you with, Mr. Sweeney?" Magnolia asked, her defensive tones reflecting her displeasure of his interactings with Louella.

Sweeney's right brow arched. "I simply wanted to discuss my former offer to buy your estate," he said precisely.

"I'm not sure. . .not sure I still. . .still want to sell it." *Especially not to you,* she added to herself. The fact that the man owned a string of saloons had certainly been a mark against him. But the longer Magnolia considered his kicking out the destitute Louella, the more she wanted to find another buyer.

"Miss Alexander, have I in some way offended you?" Sweeney leaned against his saddle horn, his lips twisting with a hint of mockery.

The crunch of Levi's footfalls just behind Maggie preceded his supportive hand on her shoulder by only seconds. His touch gave her the courage she needed to defend Louella. "No, you have done nothing to me personally, but you certainly offended a friend of mine—Louella Simpson."

Once more his brow arched, and he took a long draw on the cigar before removing it from his teeth to study the smoking tip.

"From what I understand," Maggie continued as the pungent odor of cigar smoke encircled her, "you dismissed her on the spot without so much as giving her the money she was rightly due." Fully expecting a heated retort, Magnolia braced herself, and Levi's grip on her shoulder increased.

Sweeney looked up from the cigar, a calculating, although humorous, gleam in his eyes. "So if I pay Louella Simpson, will you reconsider my offer?"

"I. . ." Never expecting Sweeney's ready cooperation, Maggie stared at him in disbelief. "I. . ."

"I'm a fair man, Miss Alexander," Sweeney said. Taking a final draw on the cigar, he tossed it onto the road and exhaled the smoke toward the west pasture. "The problem with *Mizz Louella* was that she and that weak-kneed manager of mine had hidden her pregnancy from me for months. I don't come through often, and she had managed to stay behind that bar when I was there. But I have a few rules concerning the people I employ—and my rules don't allow *pregnant* women. It ain't right for a pregnant woman to be working in a saloon. It's bad for her and bad for business."

A bit flustered with his improper use of such a word, Maggie looked at his horse's well-manicured hooves and couldn't believe for one second that Jed Sweeney cared at all about Louella's well-being.

"Excuse me for interrupting. . ." Removing his hand from her shoulder, Levi stepped to Maggie's side, his tone suggesting he didn't appreciate the saloon owner's language any more than Magnolia did. "But I am now considering the purchase of Miss Alexander's property. I'm sure she will let you know if she reconsiders your offer."

Shocked by Levi's words, Magnolia forced herself to stare at her fingers, now intertwined in a tight knot.

Silence followed. The kind of silence that suggests mute fury. Maggie looked up to see Sweeney's eyes narrowed to thin slits. All humor, all mockery were replaced by rage. "I offered first," he growled.

"Mr. Sweeney, I never promised I'd sell to you," Maggie firmly stated.

As slow as a listless copperhead, Sweeney reached into his breast pocket and pulled out a brass money clip, holding a thick stack of bills. With the flip of his wrist, he coldly tossed a ten-dollar bill onto the ground between them. "That's more than enough to make *Mizz Louella* happy," he said in an expressionless tone, which belied the anger, still stirring his eyes. "I'll be by the boardinghouse Monday in hopes that you'll change your mind about the estate." He disdainfully observed the injured Levi. "Takes money to buy a spread like this, Miss Alexander, and many times a hopeful buyer can't pull together the funds. Might better reconsider my offer while I'm in the buying vein." Without another word, he yanked the stallion's reins to the left and galloped back toward the road.

"We need to continue our journey to your brother's ranch," Magnolia said, grabbing the ten-dollar bill and marching toward the buggy before Levi had a chance to so much as utter one word.

❧

Narrowing his eyes, Levi watched her stiffly mount the buggy and turn an expressionless, blue gaze his way, as if she were impatiently awaiting him to follow. So much had happened in this journey with Magnolia that he felt as if he needed at least two nights on the range to sort it all out. He thought about that blasted wall she had erected between them. Somehow, that little lady had managed to get scared stiff of any kind of a relationship. She had only made vague references of something to do with her family. Levi wondered if it all related to her uncle's murder.

Nevertheless, he recalled the moments she had let down her guard. She had enjoyed his winking at her that very morning. Levi reveled in the memory of her in his arms, and his pulse quickened with the expectation of a possible commitment in days to come. For during all those long hours Levi had lain in that doctor's bed, he had prayed. He had prayed as he had never prayed in his life. And, he at last came to the conclusion that Miss Magnolia Alexander was the answer to his prayers for a godly wife. But Levi had also felt a heavenly caution that these things take time.

He shouldn't rush Magnolia. He *wouldn't* rush Magnolia. Levi would continue praying, continue chipping away, bit by bit, at that wall of hers. Continue in tenacious persistence. Magnolia might not realize it, but Levi Camp-bell had chased stray dogies across the plains longer than he had chased her.

He produced what he hoped was his most engaging smile and stepped toward Magnolia, perched upon that buggy. But he paused and glanced back toward the lane, toward the place where Jed Sweeney had disappeared from view. With a knot of dislike forming in his gut, Levi decided he would purchase this place before allowing the likes of that hardened saloon owner to buy the home where Magnolia grew up. And what that Sweeney fellow didn't know was that Levi had more than enough money in his trust fund to pay for the estate. The plan hatching in his mind left him smiling all the broader. He would buy Magnolia's old home place. Then, he would win her heart.

During the fifteen-minute journey to Travis and Rachel's ranch, Levi chose to remain silent. He stared straight ahead at the rutted lane. He never once gave Magnolia cause for discomfort, although Levi felt her discomfort—felt it as thick as that bitter brew he and Dr. Engle enjoyed that morning. Only one fact stopped Levi from drowning in confusion over Magnolia's vacillating responses to him. She *did enjoy* his embrace. Levi only had to somehow break through that stone bulwark she continued to erect between them.

"There's Travis and Rachel's place—just up ahead." Maggie pointed toward a new white barn rising above the pasture where four Appaloosas grazed. Near the barn, Levi caught glimpses of a ranch house with a broad front porch.

"Travis wrote us about the barn burning and all the trouble Rachel had with that horrible neighbor. But looks like they did a fine job of buildin' a new barn." Thankful for any topic of conversation that he could share with Magnolia, Levi admired the lush, green countryside and rolling pastures. "You know, in Travis's letters, he said the place looked like a green paradise, but it's mighty strange to see rolling hills and all these trees in Texas. Around El Paso, all we have are flatlands."

"Local folks have reason to boast about the scenery." As she turned the horses onto the lane leading to the ranch house, now clearly in view, Maggie thoughtfully appraised the land, a faint wisp of indecision flitting across her features. "I do love the home where I grew up," she said wistfully. "I only wish I had the skills to run a ranch. . . ."

"I meant what I said back there, Magnolia," Levi said. "I would be honored for you to sell your uncle's property to me."

Startled, she observed him as if she were searching for any traces of teasing. "But there's over two hundred and fifty acres there. . .and all the cattle. . .and the crops and the whole thing is worth. . .is worth. . ."

He shrugged and produced the most flirtatious smile he could conjure up. "I've lived with cows most of my life, remember? Two hundred and fifty acres is a drop in the bucket compared to the size of my pa's ranch, and—"

A spark of ire flashed in her eyes.

"I'm not trying to belittle your holdin's in any way, now. It's a simple fact, that's all. And another simple fact is, I'll pay you top dollar. I can have the cash here by next week. There's nothin' I'd love more than ownin' a little east Texas ranch right next to my big brother's." Even as the words left his mouth, Levi wondered at his meaning. Two years ago, the last thing he would have ever wanted was to live by his older, "perfect" brother. But perhaps during this trip the Lord was helping him come to final terms with the remaining traces of jealousy left over from childhood. Even if their father couldn't quiet understand Levi's bent to poetry, his need for quietude, his desire to pen his own poems and essays, he and Levi had grown closer in the year since Travis's absence. A closeness that had resulted in the elder Campbell bequeathing Levi an equal share in the Campbell ranch with Travis.

As if Levi had never made the offer, Maggie silently guided the carriage to a stop near the expansive, white barn. With Travis trudging toward them from the rolling pasture, Levi hoped her silence stemmed from surprised consideration of his earnest offer and not from a bent to reject him.

Levi disembarked the carriage, as a red-eyed Travis approached his brother's side. The only other time Levi had ever known Travis to cry was at the death of their grandfather. Truly, the loss of that baby must be eating him up. Levi's own eyes stung at the sight of his elder brother's pain. Once again, an ocean of guilt lapped against the sands of his soul. The news of the miscarriage had come on the heels of a round of envious thoughts concerning Travis, the same types of thoughts that had plagued Levi his whole life. Yet Travis had never done anything to purposefully evoke Levi to jealousy. Levi didn't even think Travis knew about the resentment. And at that moment, standing beside his older brother, Levi vowed that with God's help he would forever divorce himself from the mental rivalry that had plagued him since birth.

"Miss Maggie." Removing his straw hat, Travis nodded toward the lady as Levi assisted her descent with his free hand. "Thanks for coming out. I know Rachel will enjoy your company. Her cousin, Angela Isaacs, is here now—"

"Yes, I know Angela well," Maggie said respectfully. "I don't know that there's much I can do. . .or say, but you and Rachel have been such a great source of support for me during my own loss, that I feel I just have to be here for you."

"We appreciate you more than you can ever know," Travis said.

She dimpled into a supportive smile. "Well, if you'll excuse me, then. . ."

With admiration flooding his every fiber, Levi watched Maggie cross the farmyard, gather her skirt, and climb the three steps onto the porch. The moment the creaky front door closed behind her, Levi turned to his elder sibling to catch an inquisitive glint in Travis's eyes, still hazy with grief.

"So the rumors around town are right?"

❧

Magnolia faintly tapped on Rachel's closed bedroom door. "Hello, Rachel?" she called gently. "It's me, Maggie. May I come in?"

A familiar face appeared on the other side of the door. "Rachel's asleep right now," Angela Isaacs whispered, "but do come in." Her chestnut-colored hair and freckled nose attested to Angela and Rachel's kinship. But that's where the cousins' similarities ended. While Rachel was fiery, Angela had always been more reclining. Angela, slender and tall, carried herself gracefully, but seemed to dwarf the petite Rachel when the two stood side by side.

Magnolia stepped into the room to see the lace curtains waving in front of the numerous bedroom windows. The large wicker fan lying on the foot of Rachel's bed attested to Angela's having fanned her cousin while she slept.

"How is she doing, Angela?" Maggie asked.

"Well, she cried herself to sleep." Angela paused to blink back the tears. "But I believe the elixir Dr. Engle left this morning has helped her sleep in peace now for the first time since the labor started last night. She's been asleep a couple of hours now."

"Bless her," Maggie said, astounded at how drawn Rachel's pale face appeared. And the bright sunshine spilling through the windows only highlighted the dark circles marring her eyes. Once again, Maggie was reminded that she didn't hold the exclusive rights to trouble. About a year ago, Rachel's father had died, leaving her alone to tend to this expansive land. Now, she and Travis had lost their first child—a little girl, according to Dr. Engle.

"Is there to be a funeral?" Magnolia asked.

"No. Travis and Dr. Engle buried the baby this morning, out in the pasture, under one of the trees."

"And Rachel? Did she see the baby?"

Angela nodded, her eyes filling with tears.

The patient stirred, and Magnolia stepped to her side to notice dots of perspiration along Rachel's forehead. "Are there some damp cloths for her face? She looks terribly hot."

"Yes," Angela said, moving to the door. "Travis just brought in a fresh bucket of cold well water not long ago. I'll go get some of it and bring some fresh cloths as well."

"Magnolia?" Rachel breathed, restlessly stirring.

"Yes, I'm here." Maggie knelt beside the feather bed and encircled Rachel's hand within her own.

At last, Rachel opened her eyes to look up at Maggie with doelike agony. "It w–was a little–little girl," she said, tears dampening her cheeks.

Remembering her own mother's pain-filled inscriptions about the deaths of her twin sons, Maggie nodded. Somehow, being with Rachel at this moment gave Maggie a sense of connection with the mother she had never known.

"Dr. Engle has–has been like a–a father to me." Rachel's voice cracked as she wrinkled her brows.

"I think he's like a father to most of Dogwood, Rachel," Maggie said. "He's a wonderful, wonderful man."

"Yes. . .but I–I can tell when–when he's withholdin' bad news. I'm afraid there's somethin' t–terribly wrong. That–that perhaps I won't ever be able–able to have children. It's just this h–horrible feelin' I have that I can't—I can't get over."

Wondering what she should say, Maggie grappled with an appropriate reply. As usual, the stirrings of inadequacy plagued her. *What do I say? How much should I tell her? Exactly how certain is Dr. Engle that Rachel mustn't try to bear children?* At last, Maggie decided that now was certainly not the time to share more disheartening news with the devastated Rachel.

"I'm not as. . .as experienced with these types of things

as Dr. Engle, but. . .but he wouldn't have left you this morning if he didn't think you were going to be fine. He'll be back out to check on you before dark this evening. You can tell him your concerns then. I'm sure he'll be glad to answer all your questions. Right now, you just need to focus on recoverin'." Maggie gripped Rachel's hand all the tighter and hoped she didn't push for more information concerning the dim prognosis.

Spiritlessly, Rachel stared out one of the open windows. "I know I sh–shouldn't doubt the–the Lord, Maggie," she said, her voice gaining strength the more she talked. "But I think I must be the worst doubter in the world. Sometimes I just don't understand why He allows all the sufferin' and. . . and death. I didn't think I'd ever get over Pa's death. Now. . . now this!" She turned imploring eyes to Maggie. "Doesn't the Lord think we would make good parents? Is there something I've done wrong? I want a baby more than anything. And if. . .if—just supposin' I can't—I'll feel as if I've let Travis down in the worst of ways."

"Yes, I understand, but. . .I'm sure the Lord will somehow. . ." Maggie didn't know what to say. So fresh were her own questions about God and life that she could do nothing but hold Rachel's hand and silently support this childhood friend. "I'll certainly keep you in my prayers," Maggie encouraged. "If. . .if you'll remember me as well."

Rachel nodded in understanding. "We can be a support to one. . .one another." Her head tilted to the side. Her heavy eyes closed. And her breathing became more steady.

Praying for Rachel's strength and her own wisdom, Magnolia thoughtfully observed her friend, slipping into the folds of sleep. And with the cattle's soft lowing flowing through the opened windows, an idea, like a tiny cloud, presented itself on the horizon of her mind. At a breathtaking pace, that cloud gained size. . .size and definite plausibility.

Louella Simpson was due to give birth very soon. She had no idea what she was going to do once the baby arrived. She had no means of supporting the child. She even said that returning to her hometown would heap ridicule upon her mother and herself. So she couldn't even go back home. But just suppose. . .just suppose Louella loved her child so much she would be willing to place it in Rachel's welcoming arms? Precious few people in Dogwood knew about Louella. Only key people had privy to the fact that Rachel had even miscarried. Rachel and Travis could very easily accept Louella's baby as their own, and the child would never bear the shame of the label "illegitimate." No one in Dogwood need ever know the child was adopted.

The sound of Angela entering the room disrupted Maggie's thoughts, but by no means dismissed the exciting possibilities. . .if only Louella would agree.

"I'm sorry it took so long," Angela said in her usually tranquil tones. "But Travis and his brother. . .um. . ." She squinted as if she were searching for his name.

"Levi," Maggie supplied while Angela poured the cool water into the stoneware washing bowl on the bedside table.

"Yes, Levi." Angela's brown eyes glittered with the romantic speculations that Magnolia had seen all over town. Was no one in Dogwood left without knowledge of Magnolia's personal life? "The two of them were inquiring concerning Rachel," the schoolteacher said. Her words, as precise as always, reflected her studious nature and the academic excellence to which she pushed her students.

"I'm so hot," Rachel muttered, stirring from her light sleep.

Maggie dipped one of the clean, although stained, cloths into the well's icy water and gently patted Rachel's forehead.

"Thank you," Rachel mumbled. Taking the cloth from Maggie, she stroked her neck and cheeks as well. "It's so p–powerfully hot today." She produced a languid smile, which hinted at her usually playful nature. "I heard you. . . talking about Levi," she said, her voice once more gaining strength with each word she spoke. "Angela, Levi is c–courting Maggie. Did you know?"

Shocked, Magnolia glanced from Rachel to the speculative Angela and back to Rachel.

"We're. . .we're going to be sisters-in-law, I think," Rachel continued.

"Yes, that's what I hear," Angela said in a scheming voice. "Yesterday at the quilting bee—"

"We aren't courting," Maggie blurted, recalling Levi's brief embrace, which suggested the opposite.

"Then may. . .maybe he'll court Angela." Rachel's feeble wink left Maggie glad to see some of the redhead's spunk, although her chagrin increased all the more.

"Even from her sickbed, she torments me," Angela said. "I'm an old maid, and I will remain that way all my years. I'll probably go to my death before trusting a man again."

"Ah, Angela, one d–day somebody as good as my Trav's gonna come along and. . .and make you forget you ever said that." Rachel raised her head and Maggie automatically placed another pillow behind her. Perhaps the patient would even feel like sipping some broth for her noon meal.

Glancing toward the blanching Angela, Maggie recalled the tragic story beneath the sudden stoniness in her eyes. She had been jilted ten years before, when Maggie was still in adolescence. Now thirty, the mildly attractive schoolteacher stood little chance at matrimony, and spinsterhood apparently suited her.

Trust. Trust. Trust. The word reverberated through Maggie's mind like an annoying chant. In recent days, she had experienced much of what she now saw in Angela's eyes. Disillusionment. Betrayal. Suspicion of all mankind. But was that any way to live? In the deepest recesses of her soul, a Still, Small Voice urged Maggie to relinquish all the anger, all the betrayal, all the uncertainties to the Lord.

eleven

After the noon meal, Maggie guided the team of sorrel mares toward Dogwood, past Uncle Cahill's estate, past neighboring farms, across the lush, rolling hills. Maggie didn't say a word to Levi, who likewise maintained a distant silence. The uneasiness of their other encounters seemed to have eased into companionable serenity. Certainly, Magnolia was beginning to comprehend that she must come to terms with some of the negative feelings that had flooded her soul upon learning of her uncle's betrayal. But even now, her heart burned with anger at the man who had raised her in the bowels of deception.

As they approached the lane leading to the Dogwood community church, she turned to her quiet traveling companion. His drawn face attested to the seriousness of the wound from which he still recovered. "I know you are tired, Levi, but could we pause for just a moment so I can visit Uncle Cahill's grave? I. . .there are some things I feel I need to talk to the Lord about."

"I think that's a good idea." His expectant gaze caressed her as a hint of a smile played on his face. "After your delicious lunch and that catnap, I'm feeling fit as a fiddle."

"Are you sure? You're looking a bit tired."

"I'm fine. You just do whatever you need to do." His grin increased to the dapper variety, and Magnolia wondered if he might be going to wink at her again.

The serenity they had just shared was dashed aside by the fresh tension now wedging itself between them. Maggie relived their brief embrace from only hours before. All the yearning, which had built from the moment she met Levi, descended upon her with renewed intensity. Before discovering Uncle Cahill's deception, Maggie had vaguely wondered if God were placing Levi in her life. But as late as this morning, Maggie had doubted Levi's constancy, were he to learn of Uncle Cahill's shameful past. Immediately, Angela Isaac's stony, distrustful face ingrained itself upon Maggie's mind. Was that the kind of lonely life she wanted? As she steered the mares toward the white, steepled church, she accepted the fact that she needed God's guidance, His healing, as never before.

A hushed tranquillity enveloped the churchyard when Maggie pulled the horses to a halt. The white house of worship thrust its steeple toward the cloudless blue sky as if to point all who passed to the Holy Creator. A warm breeze stirred the summer heat and wafted the smells of bitterweeds and pines across the green hills. Intent on soaking up the peacefulness, Maggie gazed toward the church where she had worshipped as a child. Now, she attended one of the churches in Dogwood, but this small sanctuary had been so much more than just a place to be on Sundays. This house of God had been the grounds on which Maggie's firm devotion to the Lord had taken root.

Uncle Cahill had made certain Maggie attended every service. Uncle Cahill had encouraged her to read the Bible. Uncle Cahill had begun every day on his knees in prayer. Despite the fact that the man was actually no kin to Maggie, he had followed closely to the Lord and had shown Maggie the Way.

From the left, Levi cleared his throat. Startled from her concerns, she looked down to see Levi standing, his left hand extended toward her. She had been so engrossed in her musings that she failed to hear him disembark the carriage. And now he stood, ready to assist her descent. This morning he had likewise extended his hand. This morning his fingers had covered hers as she stepped from the buggy. This morning he had embraced her and pleaded that she tell him the reasons for her impassioned aversion to his courting her. Would Levi repeat the embrace from only hours ago?

❧

Magnolia, her blue eyes stirring with confusion, placed her hand into Levi's. As much as he wanted to feel her in his arms, Levi backed away to give her plenty of space to disembark. She stepped onto the dusty churchyard, and Levi couldn't resist holding her hand several seconds longer than necessary, pausing in appreciation of her beauty. That blond hair, with wisps forever curling around her face. The fires of faith burning in her soul. The way those dimples formed when she smiled. Magnolia returned his appraisal, and for the first time since she erected that wall of ice between them, Levi perceived that it might very well be melting. He had been transparent in his desires to court her. Perhaps she was coming to terms with the unexplained fears that sprang between them.

Turning her face toward the graveyard, she removed her hand from his.

"I'll wait in the church," he said.

Nodding, she walked the short distance to the cemetery,

the summer wind swishing her skirts around her ankles. Levi tethered the horses to a nearby tree, then paused with his hand on the stair rail leading into the clapboard building. Pensively, he watched Maggie kneel beside a fresh grave. *Oh Father*, he pleaded silently. *Help her.*

Entering the country chapel, Levi's footsteps echoed across the empty sanctuary. Through the dozen tall windows lining the room, spears of sunlight warmed the air, which smelled of musty hymnbooks. The sound of Levi's boots against polished wooden floors echoed off the ceiling as he walked down the center aisle. He stepped between the pews only long enough to open several of the windows in an effort to circulate the hot, stale air. At last, he reached the point of his destination. The well-worn mourner's bench. Bracing himself with his left arm, Levi knelt in front of the tear-stained altar and wondered how many men before him had sought the Lord for divine guidance here.

In an attempt to gain a comfortable position, he adjusted the Colt .45 Peacemaker encased in its soft leather holster, which Travis had returned during their visit. Oddly, the firearm he had worn as an extension of himself now left him a bit awkward after days without it. For several long minutes, Levi rested on his knees. Soaking in the stillness. Focusing his thoughts on nothing in particular. Feeling peacefully at ease. This trip to Dogwood, which started as a harmless journey to visit his elder brother, had turned into a life-changing event. For the first time in his life, Levi had been shot. For the first time, he had met a godly woman with whom he had shared a reciprocal attraction. For the first time, he had offered to buy his own ranch. A ranch that belonged to the woman of his dreams. Surely, Levi required divine guidance now more than ever.

Accompanied by the sounds of a distant woodpecker pounding his way into a tree, Levi began his prayer. "Lord. You promise to give wisdom to anyone who asks, and I'm asking You now. What would You have me do? You know I've prayed about this before, but I'm asking now if maybe my human desires are jumping in the way of Your will. I think I know myself well enough to say that I'll do whatever You ask of me—only show me, Lord, what that might be."

A wisp of a breeze seemed to carry his words heavenward as he continued his petition. "I'm not skilled enough in the ways of women to understand what's going on in Magnolia's heart. But You created her. You must know what she needs. I'm begging You, Father. Show me Your will! Give me wisdom in dealing with her."

Once again, Levi allowed his mind to drift aimlessly. He looked out an open window to the shaded cemetery situated on the churchyard's western slope. Maggie's huddled form crouched beside her uncle's fresh grave. Her shoulders shook with inaudible sobs.

"Lord," Levi prayed. "Please put your arms around Magnolia and draw her near to You." He paused, then slowly said, "And if I am *not* the one to help in her healing, won't You bring another man into her life that she can trust to help carry her burdens." The last words were some of the hardest Levi had ever prayed. Even though he had talked to the Lord many an hour while in that bed of recovery, and even though he had felt nothing but a deep peace that Magnolia's presence was something the Lord had planned, Levi experienced a new release from the whole situation. A release he had not known since the first time he began to grasp the dream of courting Miss Magnolia Alexander. Certainly, Levi was placing his "angel of mercy" into the Hands that had created her and abandoning himself to God's sovereign will. Whether that be marriage to Maggie or life alone on a west Texas ranch, Levi would accept God's plan.

As he once more observed Magnolia's battling her overwhelming grief, a compulsion to wrap his arms around her in comfort overtook Levi and bade him to approach her. Purposefully, he rose from his place of prayer and retraced his earlier steps. After closing the windows, he left the church and took determined strides across the yard as the urgency to be with Magnolia grew.

Her sobs, accompanied by that persistent woodpecker, echoed through the tombstones as Levi neared. At once, Levi second-guessed his decision to intrude on this private moment. But the former desire to comfort her pushed him forward once more.

"Uncle Cahill, why weren't you honest with me from the beginning?" Magnolia demanded through broken sobs.

Levi stopped again as he considered the meaning of her painful outburst.

"This would all be so much easier if I had dealt with it when you were still alive."

Gently, Levi laid a supportive hand on Magnolia's shoulder and knelt beside her.

Covering her face, she turned into his embrace, her wrenching cries now muffled against his shirt. In silence, Levi rested his head atop hers and groped for a way to comfort the seemingly inconsolable woman.

"What has you so troubled, Magnolia? Won't you please tell me? There seems to be more to your grievin' than your uncle's death. And I can't help you if I don't know what's wrong."

"Oh, Levi," she said, pulling away to expose him to tear-filled eyes. "Uncle Cahill was nothing but a fraud and a liar and a coward to boot! It wasn't until he was faced with his death that he had the courage to write a letter and confess the truth to me." And Magnolia poured out the full story of what she had so recently learned: James Calloway, alias Cahill Alexander, was an impostor.

On a shuddering breath, she finished her sorrowful report. "And now I'm going to have to witness in court against that horrible man in jail and the whole county will know I was raised by an outlaw. It's going to ruin me! No one will want to walk on the same side of the street with me. No upright man would ever marry me!"

"Is *this* the reason you keep pushing me away?" Within Levi's heart, a blossom of exultation sprouted where only confusion had once grown.

"Yes, partly," she said, brushing away the final tears.

Spontaneously, Levi threw back his head and laughed as if he were alone on the west Texas range.

"This is not funny!" Placing hands on hips, Magnolia stamped her foot.

"Oh yes, it is!" he said, shaking his head. "Long ago I think my mother decided I was a hopeless cause in the ways of society. When I wouldn't follow Travis's footsteps and be shipped off to that stuffy law school in Boston, I think they just 'bout gave up on me.

" 'What will people think?' I heard my mother say that more times than not. But, I'd always just shrug my shoulders and ride onto the range with my poetry books and journal."

"You write?" Magnolia asked, blinking in surprise.

"Of course." He winked jauntily and watched with delight as her cheeks flamed to that enchanting shade of crimson. "I've even been guilty of composing a few poems for one pretty little lady in Dogwood."

Her cheeks grew all the redder, and she stood to step away from him. "That's all fine and good, Mr. Campbell," she said formally. "And you can make light of my concerns all you want, but—"

He closed the few feet that separated them and gently grasped her upper arm. "I'm tellin' you, Magnolia. I don't care what your uncle was or wasn't. I'm interested in getting to know *you*."

"But people will—"

"I'm not the kind of man to put stock in what anybody thinks."

She searched his face as if she were searching for any signs of falsehood in his claim.

"I understand the reason you would think that about me," he said diplomatically. "There's some people who—who are so bent on what others think they'd throw away their own lives for the sake of pleasing the world. But that's not the kind of man I am, Magnolia." He stroked her cheek with the back of his fingers and cherished its softness. "All I'm askin' is that you consent to givin' the two of us time to get to know one another. Will you let me call on you?"

Staring down at her knotted fingers, she hesitated. "There's more to it than just that." Her nostrils flaring, she raised her chin and boldly held his gaze. "How do I know I can trust you?" she blurted. "The one man I thought would never betray me has done exactly that!" Maggie pointed toward the grave, covered in red dirt. "He wasn't even who he *said* he was."

Levi blinked with the vehemence of her words as a heavenward plea formed in his soul. A plea for wisdom. "I guess," he finally said, "you'll just have to give me the chance to prove I'm trustworthy. At least I am who I say I am, you know that much. You have Travis's word on that."

"And you would stand by me through public disgrace?"

"Every minute of it."

"And you wouldn't care that people might say you are the same kind of man Uncle Cahill used to be?"

"No. I am who I am in Christ. And He's teaching me not to lean so much on what everyone thinks." Levi hesitated before expounding on this new vein of contemplation. With another heavenward cry for help, he continued, "And I think that's something your uncle Cahill learned as well. There's a verse that I've clung to many a nights out under the stars: 'Therefore if any man be in Christ, he is a new creature: old things are passed away; behold, all things are become new.' "

Her pale blue eyes flashed with the sparks of astonishment. Astonishment and a glimmer of understanding. Understanding and eagerness. An eagerness to hear more of what Levi was saying.

"Sounds to me like your uncle made some wrong decisions, even after he accepted Christ. But he still followed the Lord and raised you to know Him. He *did* become a new man in Christ. Just like we have.

"I think when your uncle found you, he was forced to make some pretty tough choices in a few moments' time, and he did the best he could under the circumstances. He didn't do so bad by you, did he? Would you have rather he turned you over to the crooked lawman to be carted off to some orphanage? He probably regretted not telling you the truth a million times. But do you know a single soul who lives without some regrets?"

Levi adjusted his right arm in the sling as a slow throb began to emanate from his injured shoulder.

Magnolia's skilled eyes noticed his discomfort. "Perhaps we should—"

He held up his hand and captured her gaze with his own. Deliberately, he winked again and smiled in a fashion he hoped left his musings clear. "But you haven't said I could court you yet. Do you honestly think I'm going anywhere until you agree?"

Solemnly, Magnolia held his gaze until the beginnings of a smile nibbled the corners of her mouth.

"I'm not asking for your hand in marriage. We haven't known each other anywhere long enough for that. But I would like the opportunity to better make your acquaintance. . .to sit beside you in church. . .to find out your likes and dislikes. . .to maybe even. . .fall in love," Levi said, reciting a few of the lines he had mentally composed after meeting Magnolia.

As the smile increased, she looked down and bit her bottom lip. "I think your parents were right. You should have been a lawyer. You would have won every case, for sure."

With a whoop, Levi picked her up with his good arm and twirled her around.

"Stop this! Stop this now!" she insisted, clamping her hand over her petite, black hat. "You're going to hurt yourself, and Dr. Engle's going to—"

Abruptly, he deposited her back on the ground with a decided thud. Grimacing, Levi clutched his shoulder as the pain tore down his right arm.

"I told you! I told you to stop that nonsense. Now look what you've gone and done to yourself! Dr. Engle will have your hide. . .and mine, too," she fussed, tugging him toward the buggy.

As Levi struggled to climb onto his seat, he smiled, even through the pain.

❧

While Maggie drove the short distance back to Dogwood, an image of Uncle Cahill bore upon her mind. She envisioned his laughing eyes—eyes that had always revealed the goodness and love of Jesus. She saw once again his carefree smile. She recalled his undying love for his "niece." Even though Magnolia wasn't certain the Lord had delivered her from every vestige of dismay and distrust, she knew He had spoken especially to her there by that gravesite. The verse Levi quoted was the very one that had haunted her the past few days. Perhaps the Lord was trying to teach her to focus more solely on Him and less on what others thought. Uncle Cahill became a new creature in Christ. But, so had Magnolia. And. . .so had Levi.

Furtively, Maggie eyed Levi from beneath her lashes. Even with the evidence of pain marring his face, the man's finely chiseled features spoke of both character and compassion. Yet despite all that he said—and all that she knew was right—a tendril of distrust twisted in her midsection. Certainly, the wrenching betrayal from Uncle Cahill's admission would take time to heal, but Magnolia would trust the Lord to help her trust Levi. She would not, she *could* not rush into anything as serious as marriage. But Maggie would grant to Levi what he had requested. The two of them would certainly get to know one another better.

Once they entered the outskirts of Dogwood, the horses turned instinctively down Main Street and through the bustling town. She pulled the carriage to a halt in front of the boardinghouse and Levi stifled a groan as he descended.

"You go up to your room, *now*," Maggie admonished in her disapproving nurse's voice. "I'm going to send for Dr. Engle."

He flashed her one of those impish grins, which Maggie was hastily coming to expect at the most inopportune moments. "So my angel of mercy carries a whip."

Before Maggie could formulate a rebuttal, Widow Baker opened the beveled glass door, and Louella Simpson eased her swollen form over the threshold and onto the porch. Wincing, Levi attempted to tip his hat at the ladies as they descended the stairs.

"Miss Maggie, wait! I'm so glad you're here." Sarah Baker, typically the epitome of aplomb, nervously fidgeted with her embroidered hanky. "Miss Louella is. . .is feeling dreadful since we took her to visit Dr. Engle earlier today," she whispered, casting a frenzied glance over her shoulder as Levi entered the boardinghouse. "I'm afraid the child is soon to appear. Luke—" She cleared her throat and glanced downward. "I mean, Dr. Engle said she could deliver any time. Would you mind terribly if we rode with you over to his office? Luke—Dr. Engle insisted on her delivering there. She will have no privacy here whatsoever. And—and she wants me with her at the time."

"Of course I'll take you," Maggie said, but her mind raged with curiosity, with astonishment. *Luke?* The Widow Baker had called Dr. Engle *Luke*! Since the mysterious rift in their relationship, Maggie had never known Sarah to refer to the doctor as anything more than a formal "Dr. Engle," a disdainful "That *Engle* Man," or a frustrated "That *Stubborn* Doctor." As Louella and Mrs. Baker mounted the buggy, Magnolia speculated that the Dogwood rumor mills might soon be humming with more than one romance.

twelve

In a matter of minutes, Maggie had ushered Louella and Mrs. Baker into the outer office and changed the linens on the bed Levi had vacated only that morning. Certainly, as Dr. Engle ascertained, these were busy days for the medical profession. But as Magnolia dashed around the small, austere room making certain all was spotlessly clean, one word drummed out a tattoo in her mind.

Adoption. Adoption. Adoption.

Would Louella? Would Travis and Rachel? Would God. . . could God have placed this hopeless young woman in the most unlikely of towns for the definite purpose of miraculously giving a newborn to a heartbroken couple?

The potential of such a match so filled Maggie with joy that, for the first time since her uncle's death, she forgot the burden of her own heartache. Someone stirred in the kitchen across the hallway, and Maggie fully expected to find the doctor. Humming a lullaby, she rushed toward the kitchen, dropping the linens near the washtub just inside the door.

"Dr. Engle!" she whispered.

The groggy doctor, turning from his pursuit of concocting more of that horrid coffee, attempted to stifle a yawn. "Excuse me, Maggie. I just woke up. I wasn't asleep long this morning when Sarah—I mean, Widow Baker arrived with Miss Simpson."

Sarah! Despite her valiant attempts to hide the conclusions at which she was swiftly arriving, Maggie's eyebrows rose.

Dr. Engle chuckled. "You look like none other than Bess Tucker."

"Doctor, *please,*" Maggie gasped, appalled that her lifetime friend would insinuate she could in any way resemble that nosy store owner.

"You're just like the rest of 'em, Maggie, whether you want to admit it or not. Just as interested in the latest gossip as everybody else around this town."

"And you're not?" she asked. "If I recall, you've looked at me rather oddly a few times lately."

"Well who wouldn't with the sparks flyin' between you and that Campbell man."

With a faint gasp, Maggie covered her mouth. "I almost forgot! You need to pay a visit to Levi at the boardinghouse. He. . ." She glanced out the window as she recalled the delightful moment Levi twirled in triumph. "He seems to have injured his shoulder."

"I told him to take it easy. What'd he do? Go chasing after a cow or something?" he said, his eyes dancing as they hadn't since. . .since the last time he courted Widow Baker.

"No. . ." Maggie hedged as the doctor finished filling the coffeepot with grounds. "But before you go check on Levi, you'll need to speak with. . .*Sarah* in the waiting room."

"She's here? Now?" He dropped the lid to the coffeepot.

"Yes. With Louella. I fear Louella's time is upon her. But—" Maggie bit her lip and hesitated only a moment before plunging into the subject that left her heart beating with anticipation. "When I was out visiting with Rachel today, I began to wonder. Dr. Engle, do you think Travis and Rachel would adopt Louella's baby? The poor girl has no place to go with a child. She can't go back home because—but if she were to allow the child to be adopted, she could go return to her ma—and no one would ever know. I just started thinking that—"

"No, child." Dr. Engle laid a fatherly hand on her forearm. "You weren't thinking. God was speaking to you."

Maggie's eyes misted. Her pulse accelerated. Her mind careened with the doctor's words.

"He has spoken to me as well. I have thought of almost nothing else since I examined Miss Simpson this morning."

"Rachel could even nurse the baby." Magnolia shook her head in wonder as a tear of exultation dropped to her cheek. During the last week, she had shed so many tears of sorrow that this moment of happiness seemed to somehow initiate the cleansing of her soul.

"I will go and examine the young lady again." Dr. Engle removed his wire-rimmed spectacles to press against his own reddened eyes. "If you will join me, perhaps the two of us could present the idea to Miss Simpson."

"And do you think Rachel and Travis—"

"I think Mr. and Mrs. Campbell will bless God all their remaining days."

❧

Magnolia cradled a newborn boy in her arms and stood on the Campbells' front porch with Levi and Dr. Engle, impatiently shifting their weight from foot to foot. The doctor hammered away at the door again and muttered under his breath. "I sent a message to Travis last night saying we'd be here by six-thirty. I don't know why he's not up and at 'em."

Joy bubbles gurgled from Maggie's soul, forcing her to suppress the giggles akin to those of a child on Christmas morning. As a mockingbird serenaded the morning, the sun's pink fingers grandly stretched themselves across the eastern horizon. Surely, nature itself was celebrating this amazing moment.

As Dr. Engle pounded on the door even more ferociously, Levi bent to gently pull the thin blanket away from the sleeping, redheaded infant. "I can't believe his hair's the same color as Rachel's," he whispered. "It just all seems too good to be true." Levi peered into Magnolia's eyes as if his meaning weren't limited to the adoption.

"It's all in God's plan," she said. "There's no other explanation." As he solemnly agreed, Magnolia fleetingly hoped Levi proved as steadfast as she wanted to believe. Throughout Louella's uncomplicated childbirth, Maggie had experienced intermittent spells of panic, due to the fact that she had actually agreed to Levi's courting her. But laced with the panic was always the same trace of peace. . .peace and a flurry in her midsection. Truly, Levi's dashing smile and candid nature touched a chord in Maggie that no man had yet to stir. She prayed, oh how she prayed, that she could learn to trust again with the same sweetness she once had known.

At last, a bleary-eyed Travis opened the door, his pullover shirt hanging outside his denims. "We were so excited, we didn't get to sleep until well after three. We—" He stopped and gazed at the infant in awe.

"Congratulations! It's a boy!" the doctor announced.

"A redheaded boy!" Levi beamed.

Unable to suppress the giggles a moment longer, Maggie extended the baby to his father. "Congratulations," she echoed, her eyes suddenly misting all over again.

Gingerly, Travis took the child. "My son," he said with wonder, staring into the infant's wrinkled face. On the heels of a yawn, the baby whimpered and squirmed.

"I think it's time for his feeding," Maggie said discreetly as they entered the house. "I can take him into Rachel, if you like, and assist her."

"Yes, yes, Maggie," the doctor insisted. "I don't know what I'd do without you. Don't know what I'd do."

"Would you mind if I carry him into Rachel?" Travis asked.

"No, not in the least." Meeting the sagacious gaze of the doctor, Magnolia waited near Levi as Travis cradled his son and strode down the short hallway.

Cloaked in respectful silence, Maggie and her companions settled upon the horsehair sofa and awaited Travis's return. When half an hour elapsed with no signs of Travis, the doctor suggested Maggie discreetly peek in on them.

Cautiously, Magnolia crept up the hallway to pause outside their opened bedroom door. The peaceful scene that greeted her could have been nothing but God-ordained. Father, mother, and baby. . .all dozed. The newborn child, his stomach assuredly full, rested peacefully against Rachel's chest. Tears of rapture still dampened Rachel's cheeks, and Travis radiated nothing short of jubilation, even in his sleep.

Louella had requested that she be allowed to spend the

night with her baby before sending him to the arms of his new mother, and Dr. Engle had granted her supplication. The young mother had shed a good number of tears when placing the child in Magnolia's arms one last time. She had even watched from the boardinghouse window as Magnolia and the baby rode away with the doctor and Levi. During those moments of departure, Maggie had wondered if they should have arranged to separate baby from mother, despite the hardships the two would face together. But with the morning's weak light gently spilling upon the scene before her, Magnolia knew she and the doctor had done the right thing—the thing God Himself had willed. And Louella. . .Louella would receive a full description of this touching scene, and God would bequeath to her His eternal peace.

❧

As the sun approached the western horizon, Magnolia and Levi stepped onto the porch of her childhood home. The two had stayed with Rachel and Travis all day long—Maggie, as Rachel's assistant; Levi, as Travis's confidant and brotherly supporter. In Travis's borrowed buggy, they were traveling back into town when Maggie requested they stop by the homestead.

Some invisible force seemed to be pulling her back to the place of her childhood. After learning all the truths about Uncle Cahill, Maggie had embraced the notion of selling the old ranch to anyone. . .*anyone*, even the likes of Jed Sweeney. But as the days melted into one another and the rawness of her pain lessened, Magnolia began to toy with the idea of keeping the place. Keeping it and hiring someone to manage the estate, to do the job of her uncle Cahill.

With a wistful sigh, she settled onto the porch swing and pushed against the porch with her feet. The sound of two courting whippoorwills echoed throughout the piney woods, and Magnolia toyed with the pleats in her pink cotton skirt. Despite the fact that her mourning period was not officially over, Maggie was sick to death of those hot black dresses. As the swing creaked beneath her, she wondered how many times she and Uncle Cahill had sat in this spot until the last rays of light slipped below the horizon. Even the squirrels, chasing among a nearby cluster of oaks, seemed as constant a part of the scenery as was the swing.

"Are you having second thoughts about selling the place?" With the swing still in motion, Levi clumsily claimed the spot beside her.

"Yes. I—" Spontaneously, she turned to Levi. "Instead of buyin' the place, would you be interested in living here as the manager for a while. . .until I begin to feel more like making a final decision?"

"Yes," he said as if the decision were already made for him. "I'd be glad to."

A surge of relief swept over Magnolia. "Then I could take my time about deciding whether or not to sell out. Last week I was so disgusted I was ready to sell everything, furniture included, to the first person who'd have it. But as disappointed as I've been over Uncle Cahill's deception, he was still. . .he was still—"

"He was the only father you ever knew," Levi said with wisdom. "And I think it's best for you to wait before making any big decisions—*any* decisions," he added, his meaning clear. "I was only offering to buy the ranch so soon because I thought maybe you *had* to sell, and I didn't want you to be forced into selling to that saloon owner."

Thoughts of Jed Sweeney left Magnolia suppressing a shudder, despite the evening heat. The only good thing she knew that man had done was to give Louella enough money to go back home. And that gesture was most likely done to soften Magnolia's resolve not to sell to him.

A resounding thud reverberated from inside the house, jarring Magnolia from her reverie. She exchanged a nonplussed stare with Levi.

"Are your hired hands supposed to be in your house?" he asked.

"No. And they should have gone home by now."

"Do you think a tree limb fell on the roof or—"

Another thump annihilated Levi's speculations and soon a shadowed figure moved behind the parlor window.

"Levi." Maggie gripped his arm. "I just saw a shadow. Somebody's in—"

"I saw it, too." Levi stood and touched the Peacemaker, holstered on his left thigh.

"Can you shoot left-handed?" Maggie whispered, feeling anything but protected at the moment.

"We'll see," he replied, drawing his weapon.

But the front door banged open, and Jed Sweeney stared at them down the barrel of his raised Winchester rifle. "Drop the gun," he growled, his ever-present cigar clamped firmly between his yellowed teeth.

Levi hesitated.

"Drop the gun *now*."

Her upper lip beading in perspiration, Maggie's stomach clenched into a tight knot as Levi obeyed the snake-eyed saloon owner's command.

"Both of you get in this house," he snarled, waving the gun toward the door.

Immediately, Maggie recalled that lecherous man in the jail cell. She remembered the lady bandit saying they hadn't murdered anyone. She reflected on her uncle's letter. Could Jed Sweeney also be a former lawman? If he were. . .and if he did kill Uncle Cahill. . .why would he offer to buy her property?

With Jed pointing that rifle at their backs, Maggie preceded Levi into the room that had witnessed many nights of familial pleasantries. But Sweeney had overturned every piece of furniture, had even gutted the red velvet settee and matching chair. As the cigar-smoking scoundrel slammed the door behind them and slid the bar lock into place, Maggie strained to see into her uncle's bedroom, only to witness the same chaos in his room as in the parlor.

"I waited until those stinkin' hired hands left before coming after it," he declared, the hardness in his glittering eyes as dense as granite. "But I'm determined to get my hands on it, even if I have to kill the two of you."

Levi stepped between Maggie and the gun, and her heart hammered wildly as she attempted to fathom Sweeney's intent. What exactly was he after? Was it so valuable that he would offer to buy the whole estate? So valuable that he would kill Uncle Cahill?

From behind Levi, Maggie peered over his shoulder and into Sweeney's murderous countenance. "You killed my uncle," she muttered in stunned disbelief.

Sweeney produced a chilling smile. "Of course," he said menacingly. "Now, I'm looking for the gold he cheated me out of twenty years ago." He laughed wickedly. "That stupid Calloway thought that just because I was in the sheriff's office that day that I was the lawman. Truth was, my brother was the lawman. I just happened by. Turned out to be my lucky day. I lied about my name, and the two of us struck a deal: I'd let him go free and he'd hand over the loot. I didn't find out until a year later from my own brother that there'd been a chest full of gold coins on that stagecoach Calloway robbed. I decided right then and there that I'd catch up with him one day. Imagine my surprise when I ran into him in this dumpy little town. Now, you two, all you have to do is hand over the gold. I promise. . ." He smiled like a demon. "I won't kill you. I'll just tie you up so you can sit tight while I have time to get out of the county."

"If there's any gold, Magnolia, give it to him," Levi said, glancing over his shoulder.

"There's no gold," she said, her voice ringing with a certainty that surprised even her ears. "Uncle Cahill l–left me a letter before his death. He said there was no gold."

Jed's intense stare, like a dagger of ice, pierced her to the base of her soul. The man had no feelings whatsoever. . .no feelings for anyone. "I told that stinkin' James Calloway I'd turn him into the law if he didn't either tell me where the gold was or pay me the equivalent in cash. He finally told me the gold was buried. I gave him a day to dig it up. When I came back, he tried to kill me. . .didn't work." His lips twisted wickedly.

"Now, by Calloway's own admission, I know there's gold here. If you do not tell me where it is, I will kill you, too," he said in measured tones.

"He means it," Levi said, his voice shaking.

Magnolia's mind raced with any possibilities, but she came up completely without options. She also believed there really was no gold. Maggie remembered the numerous years when the cotton crop had failed or the winter had been harsh and they had suffered financially from the loss of crops or cattle. If Uncle Cahill had been hiding gold, he would certainly have delved into it during the lean years. Instead, they had struggled past the seasons of financial difficulties until the profitable ranch now thrived. Perhaps her uncle did tell Sweeney he would dig up the fictitious gold in order to buy time. With that gun pointing in her face, Magnolia would almost tell Sweeney anything he wanted to hear, as well.

"Let's go to the barn and get some shovels," she said, sounding much calmer than she felt. With Sweeney's gun in their backs, they walked through the kitchen, to the spacious back porch, and onto the dusty barnyard. All the while, Maggie prayed. She prayed as she had never prayed in her life. She wanted a husband and children. . .a life. Furtively, she glanced toward Levi, his intense eyes reflecting her own inner turmoil. Assuredly, Maggie perceived that if something didn't happen soon, Sweeney would kill her and Levi, gold or no gold.

With the waning sun inviting evening's shadows to creep alongside the trees and hills, Maggie pushed against the massive barn door. The hinges produced a faint squeak—a squeak that reflected the hopeless whimpers floating from Maggie's soul. *Please, God, please do something! Don't let this evil man kill us!*

The rivulets of light seeping through the hayloft's ajar

door provided precious little illumination for the dark building. With the smells of hay and horse manure engulfing her, Maggie stepped into the unlit building and halted, giving her eyes a chance to adjust.

"Keep walkin'," Sweeney demanded from behind Levi.

Maggie glanced to her left, noticing the two shovels for which she came. Darting a prayer heavenward, she quickly stepped toward them, grabbed one, raised it over her head, and held her breath as first Levi, then Sweeney stepped into the barn. With a rush of strength, she crashed the shovel blade against Sweeney's temple. Only a muffled grunt passed his lips before he dropped like a bag of feed, his Winchester spinning across the dirt floor.

Levi, quick to action, retrieved the rifle and pointed it toward the murderer.

Shivering in horror, the dazed Magnolia gaped at the unconscious man sprawled at her feet. How had she conjured the courage and strength to render him powerless? But Maggie knew, even as the question of awe rushed upon her, that the strength, courage, and power had not been her own. The Lord Himself had divinely imparted these gifts to her.

In the distance, the pond frogs voiced their nightly chant. The bobwhites whistled their simple message. A mare, resting in her stall, whinnied uncertainly. And Levi looked at the trembling Maggie, a glimmer of admiration in his eyes.

"You're my kinda woman, Magnolia Alexander," he said with one of his untimely winks.

epilogue

Two years later, Maggie again settled on the porch swing and pushed against the porch with her foot. A tiny bundle claiming her arms, she smiled with a contentment only Jesus Christ could impart. The six-week-old Sarah Louella yawned and rubbed her eyes with a tiny fist, and Maggie bestowed a tender kiss against the baby's forehead. Sarah Engle, no longer the Widow Baker, and Rachel, busy with her two-year-old, had been such a help to Maggie during these first weeks of the baby's life. Dr. Engle had insisted his wife leave her duties as his nurse to stay with Maggie at least one day a week. And Travis had likewise persisted in making certain Rachel assisted their new sister-in-law. Maggie certainly couldn't have survived without the two women.

Already, the first stars appeared against the twilight sky, and Magnolia waited for Levi to join her for their nightly prayers and Bible reading. His worn, black Bible in hand, Levi strode from the house, and Maggie slowed the swing to let him claim the spot beside her. "I thank God every hour of the day for Sarah. . .and you," he said, brushing his lips against her forehead.

"I feel the same way," Maggie said. "Two years ago, I never dreamed I could be so happy."

"The Lord's healing is a marvelous thing. . .a marvelous thing."

"Yes, I think I'm learning that no matter how people might betray us, the Lord is always steadfast." Maggie reflected over the slight tinge of pain, still present when she thought of Uncle Cahill's deception. Ironically, the very man who passed onto her a legacy of trusting the Lord had himself covered the whole truth. But despite all his mistakes, she would certainly extend her uncle's legacy of faith to the next generation. With Jed Sweeney having been convicted and hanged, Maggie was putting her past behind her. Levi was steadfastly proving to the township that he and his wife were indeed worthy of respect, regardless of Cahill's scandalous past. And Maggie, day by day, was growing in her reliance on the constancy of a godly man.

A Letter To Our Readers

Dear Reader:

In order that we might better contribute to your reading enjoyment, we would appreciate your taking a few minutes to respond to the following questions. We welcome your comments and read each form and letter we receive. When completed, please return to the following:

Rebecca Germany, Fiction Editor
Heartsong Presents
PO Box 719
Uhrichsville, Ohio 44683

1. Did you enjoy reading *Texas Lady?*
   ❑ Very much. I would like to see more books by this author!
   ❑ Moderately
   I would have enjoyed it more if ________________

   ____

   ____

2. Are you a member of **Heartsong Presents**? Yes ❑ No ❑
   If no, where did you purchase this book?______________

   ____

3. How would you rate, on a scale from 1 (poor) to 5 (superior), the cover design?______________________________

4. On a scale from 1 (poor) to 10 (superior), please rate the following elements.

   _____ Heroine _____ Plot

   _____ Hero _____ Inspirational theme

   _____ Setting _____ Secondary characters

5. These characters were special because________________

____

____

6. How has this book inspired your life?________________

____

____

7. What settings would you like to see covered in future **Heartsong Presents** books?____________________

____

____

8. What are some inspirational themes you would like to see treated in future books?____________________

____

____

9. Would you be interested in reading other **Heartsong Presents** titles? Yes ❑ No ❑

10. Please check your age range:
❑ Under 18 ❑ 18-24 ❑ 25-34
❑ 35-45 ❑ 46-55 ❑ Over 55

11. How many hours per week do you read?______________

Name ____

Occupation ____

Address ____

City ________________ State __________ Zip __________